Also by Ron Schwab

Sioux Sunrise
Paint the Hills Red
Ghosts Around the Campfire

The Lockes
Last Will
Medicine Wheel

The Law Wranglers
Deal with the Devil
Mouth of Hell
The Last Hunt
Summer's Child
Peyote Spirits

The Coyote Saga
Night of the Coyote
Return of the Coyote
Twilight of the Coyote

Peyote Spirits

A Law Wranglers Novella

Ron Schwab

Uplands Press
OMAHA, NEBRASKA

Uplands Press
P.O. Box 6105
Omaha, NE 68106
www.uplandspress.com

Publisher's Note: This is a work of fiction. Names, characters, places, and incidents are a product of the author's imagination. Locales and public names are sometimes used for atmospheric purposes. Any resemblance to actual people, living or dead, or to businesses, companies, events, institutions, or locales is completely coincidental.

Ordering Information:
Quantity sales. Special discounts are available on quantity purchases by corporations, associations, and others. For details, contact the "Special Sales Department" at the address above.

Peyote Spirits/ Ron Schwab -- 1st ed.

ISBN 978-1-943421-33-6

Peyote Spirits

Chapter 1

QUANAH PARKER'S MESSENGER sat in Jael Chernik Rivers's office clad only in a breechclout and the tip of a dried buffalo tail suspended from a rawhide cord about his neck. She envied him his attire this scorching July morning near the Comanche-Kiowa reservation in Indian Territory. At least her square box of an office, located in the building's corner, offered a window on each exterior wall. Her husband Josh's identical box provided a single window. Not that an open window sucked any cool air into the offices, but it provided an outlet for some of the inside steam to escape.

"Tell me, Buffalo Tail," the slender, sable-haired lawyer said, speaking Comanche, "what is so urgent that Quanah must see me this afternoon?" Of course, Quanah could have visited her office, but, as the principal chief of the Comanche, he was accustomed to summoning. He paid too well for her to quibble over such things.

"He has asked me to summon She Who Speaks about the defense of Broken Wing and other concerns."

Jael was still known among Quanah's Kwahadi band by her Comanche name. "I remember Broken Wing. He is a young brave of no more than eighteen winters. Why does he require defending?"

"He is being held in the soldiers' guardhouse. It is said he murdered a woman."

"Not Broken Wing? I remember him as a very kind and gentle young man."

"Agreed. Such a killing would seem contrary to his nature."

"I hear doubt in your voice."

"He was found naked and in a deep trance on the floor of the woman's bedroom. The woman lay dead on her bed. She had been stabbed many times."

"She was a white woman?"

"Yes. A sergeant's wife. They lived in the building for such married officers."

"Do you know her name?"

"They call her Mollie."

Mollie Day. First Sergeant Colin Day's wife. A pert, blonde young woman, barely twenty years old. She and other enlisted men's wives handled much of the laundry for the Rivers household, a more profitable sideline than their usual laundry services for Fort Sill soldiers. Her face always wore a welcoming smile, contrasting sharply with her burly husband's sober, often grumpy, demeanor. Mollie had made her appearance on the post six months earlier when the Irish sergeant returned from furlough with a petite bride half his age. The match had set the gossips' tongues wagging, but Mollie's friendly, outgoing personality quickly smothered the talk, and she wormed her way into the hearts of most who came to know her. This was terrible news.

Jael said, "I will go to the reservation this afternoon. I should try to see Broken Wing first. You said he was in a trance. Do you mean he was unconscious? Had he been struck down?"

"No. This is for Quanah to explain. You must not speak with Broken Wing until after you meet with Quanah."

The Kwahadi warrior stood and walked out of the room, stopping briefly in the reception area to speak softly with Rabbit, the Rivers and Sinclair firm's young Kwahadi secretary. Jael leaned back in the oak swivel chair her Cherokee friend, Oliver Wolf, had crafted and swung it around to face the window that opened to the west. She gazed at the undulating waves of seemingly endless browning grass. Occasional funnels of red dust swept across the prairie, stirring up even more dirt in their passing. A rain would be welcome, but she loved this land some might call desolate. In her heart she was still Comanche.

She wondered if Josh would return tonight. He had ridden to the Texas Panhandle and Palo Duro Canyon country to negotiate a major cattle purchase for Quanah. The Comanche chief had decided to plunge seriously into the cattle business. The Comanche elders leased most of the reservation land to nearby cattle ranchers, but Quanah, the astute capitalist, planned to stock part of the land with a Comanche herd that included some of his private bovines. The Kwahadi, the last holdouts, had arrived at Signal Station June 2, 1875, and Quanah had moved quickly to make his place in the white man's world. A natural politician, he curried the favor of the white military and bureaucrats and forged a fast friendship with Fort Sill's commanding officer, Colonel Ranald Slidell Mackenzie, a Civil War brevet general, his one-time nemesis.

It had been more than three years now since settlement of the Kwahadi at Fort Sill and her own marriage to

Josh Rivers. During that time Jael had read and studied the law with Josh's firm headquartered in Santa Fe, and in March passed the bar examination and was admitted to practice law in the federal courts, as well as any local courts of the New Mexico and Indian territories. She and Danna Sinclair, who was managing partner at the Santa Fe office, were the only women lawyers engaged in practice in the Southwest.

Jael was grateful now for the time spent with Martin Locke, the lawyer who handled most of the criminal and trial work at the Santa Fe office. There was no more skilled advocate than Marty, and Buffalo Tail's message suggested a monumental testing of her own skills.

Enough musing. Time to get to work. She sighed and got up and walked into the reception area where Rabbit pecked at the sole Remington typewriter in the office. A recently purchased manual on typing mechanics was spread out on the desk, and it seemed that the pecking pace had picked up the past few days.

"Is the book helping?" Jael asked.

The girl looked up and smiled. She was eighteen years old but a tiny thing who could pass for several years younger. Sparkling blue eyes confirmed her half-blood status. A brown tint to her hair also came from her mother, a white captive abducted as a child and raised among the Kwahadi. Comanche was a culture and way of life, not a race, Jael thought. Jael's birth parents were German Jews, but, after their murder by Comanche attackers, Jael, at age fourteen, had been carried off and soon carved her own place in the band as Quanah's interpreter and, later, counselor. Because of her gift for languages, she had been named She Who Speaks. She was verbally fluent in English, German, Hebrew, Yiddish, Spanish, and Comanche. Only since arriving at Fort Sill had she perfected her reading and writing of Spanish, and Comanche, of course, defied a written version. Jael struggled when she ferreted out a few hours to develop a phonetic dictionary that might be used by English speakers to communicate conversationally with Comanche.

Rabbit said, "I am learning to place and move my fingers, but I still must look at the letters on the keyboard. I will learn."

"I know you will. Josh will probably have contracts for you to type when he returns. Don't let him rush you. Take your time and try to type the way the manual teaches."

"That will be fun. And Josh will not rush me. He is very patient and always kind."

The women all loved Josh, Jael thought. Fortunately, he seemed unaware of his charm. "He is a kind man," Jael conceded. "His patience is not quite so consistent."

"I had a proposal this morning," Rabbit said, blushing noticeably.

"A proposal?"

"Buffalo Tail said he would like to have me as his third wife."

"I hope you declined."

"I told him I would consider only if he divorced the other two. And, of course, he would not do that. They have given him many children."

"Good. The Washington government is pushing to end polygamy in the tribes. And you would not be happy as a third wife."

"You were a third wife," Rabbit reminded her.

"Yes. And I loved Four Eagles. After the soldiers killed him, I grieved for months. But I hated it when he shared a buffalo robe at night with his other wives. Sometimes I dreamt of their deaths so I could be his only woman. It was also difficult because the other wives disliked me."

Rabbit giggled. "Probably because he came to your robe most."

Jael could not deny it but thought it best to change the subject. "I must ride out to meet with Quanah this afternoon. I am going to eat something and change into my riding clothes. Michael is already at the reservation playing with friends. If I can find him, I will bring him home with me. Otherwise, if he returns before I do, please tell him he is to remain here until I get back."

"I will do that. I am sure he will find a book to read."

"And, Rabbit, it appears Broken Wing will soon be our client. I will explain later, but be alert to anything you hear about him."

"Broken Wing? He is so handsome. I would be his first wife."

Chapter 2

JAEL ENTERED THE family living quarters from the door that opened from the office to the residence. Rivers and Sinclair had purchased the two-story, native limestone structure that housed both personal and professional spaces. Oliver Wolf had designed and supervised the renovation of the abandoned house, and Jael could not imagine more elegant surroundings. Of course, her basis for comparison was largely the Comanche tipi that had seemed more than adequate during her years on the open prairies. The house and nearby stable erupted stark and lonely from the table-flat land that unfolded more than a mile from the outskirts of Fort Sill to the east. Jael treasured the solitude that the place shared with their winter residence located in the bluffs several miles outside Santa Fe.

She climbed the stairway to the second floor, which included the spacious bedroom she shared with Josh at one end of the hall and two smaller bedrooms, one of which was claimed by nine-year old Michael. The other was set aside for their foster daughter, Rylee O'Brian, who had just turned seventeen and lived most of the time at their Santa Fe residence. Rylee, a young woman with exceptional business instincts and mathematical skills, worked at the Second National Bank under the supervision of Willi Spiegelberg, one of five brothers who operated the bank and the largest mercantile store in the Southwest. The tall, gangly string-bean had blossomed into a gorgeous rose, but her obsession with things business appeared to have rendered her ignorant of her impact on the other sex. She worried about Rylee living alone in the Santa Fe house when she and Josh were absent, but she reminded herself that her husband's sister, Tabitha, and Oliver Wolf resided a long stone's throw away in their new home.

In her bedroom Jael quickly kicked off her uncomfortable, high-button shoes and shucked the gray gabardine dress and cumbersome undergarments and plucked a blue cotton shirt and buckskin riding britches from the closet. She also snatched up a pair of ankle-high moccasins and soon felt like one of The People again. She hurried back down the stairs and grabbed her Winchester before heading for the stable.

Chapter 3

JAEL TIED HER dun gelding, Trouble, at one of the hitching rails that lined one side of the principal chief's cluster of tipis. The spirited horse was a contrary animal, big, well-muscled and thick chested, given to rebellion, and she loved him. A warrior's horse.

Quanah, known as Quanah Parker since adopting the surname of his mother Cynthia Ann's family, had set his tipis off some distance from others in the vicinity, befitting a chief of his standing. The Comanche concept of village, originally structured for defense and community survival, was rapidly dissipating. Family groups had started separating from the main body of The People and taking up residence elsewhere on the vast reservation lands.

Buffalo Tail spotted Jael and rushed out to intercept her as she walked deliberately toward the tipis. He waved her toward the largest tipi centered in the scattering of nearly a dozen. An American flag fluttered on a crudely-hewn pole near the opening, signaling this was what Quanah Parker considered his official office. She followed Buffalo Tail through the entrance and found the former Kwahadi war chief sitting on a buffalo robe, wearing a white shirt and scarlet kerchief with his buckskin leggings and moccasins. A fabric matching the kerchief intertwined with his long braids.

Quanah could have been nothing but a chief, Jael thought, tall with chiseled facial features and an aristocratic bearing that made him stand out in any gathering of people. His white blood did not show in flawless skin that was darker than that of most Comanche. His handsome, solemn face, on which she had rarely seen a smile, and his penetrating gray-blue eyes suggested a keen intelligence, and she knew him to be a man of vision and unsurpassed political and business skills.

The war chief's transition to the world of his mother's roots had been planned before the peace. Quanah had even retained Josh Rivers as his attorney to negotiate and lay groundwork, Josh unaware at the time his captive son was living in the village under the care of a new mother called She Who Speaks.

Quanah nodded for her to be seated on the robe across the cold fire pit from him. Speaking Comanche, he instructed Buffalo Tail to leave. Jael could see this did not please the warrior, but he dared not protest if he wished to continue as one of Quanah's hangers-on. Some who lacked the skills to lead, she observed, gloried in the shadow of the leader. She supposed all great men found their fawning toadies useful on occasion.

"No talk the American now. This business of The People."

Quanah was making admirable progress in learning English, even enlisting a tutor from one of the several church-sponsored schools on the reservation to work with him on reading and writing. Another example of his wisdom, Jael thought. But they did not have time to wade through his broken English. She replied in Comanche. "I am told you wish my help with Broken Wing."

"Yes. You have been told he is accused of killing a white woman?"

"Buffalo Tail told me only that the woman had been stabbed to death, and Broken Wing was found in her sleeping place."

"General Mackenzie sent a lieutenant to tell me of Broken Wing's arrest. He will be a prisoner of the Army and his guilt or innocence is to be decided by soldiers. I do not want this. He should be given up to The People to determine his fate. I want you to bring Broken Wing to me."

Jael knew Quanah was asking the impossible, but she sensed the chief was not telling all he knew. "I must be told all that you know about this. How did Broken Wing come to be at the woman's lodge?"

"He had a vision."

"A vision?"

"At the meeting of the Peyote Religion last night, followers gathered at the peyote lodge to seek the Great Spirit's guidance on our journey into the white man's world. As you know, I am the roadman for the Comanche believers. Broken Wing attended his first meeting and partook of too many buttons, I fear."

Before the Kwahadi surrender, Jael had attended a meeting, one of the few women invited to do so. She had eaten the bitter buttons harvested from the tops of peyote cactuses, undergoing a frightening experience she declined to repeat. The psychedelic effects had taken her back to the murder of her parents by the Comanche, which she had suppressed in her mind until the night of the ritual. Quanah's status as roadman compared to a high priest that might be found in other religions.

She asked, "Are you suggesting the peyote is related to his arrest?"

"The buttons first made Broken Wing very sick. He stumbled outside the ceremonial tipi and the the contents of his belly spewed upon the earth. Then he returned and collapsed and fell into a long sleep. When he awakened, he announced that the Great Spirit had told him this soldier's woman, Mollie, was to be his guide along the white man's trail. I warned him that dreams and visions brought forth by the peyote required deep thought, as they often meant something different than a brave or warrior might first assume. Sometimes it takes many meetings with the peyote to discover the true meaning of the revelation. But the young sometimes do not have the patience to pursue the journey to truth, which can be a difficult thing to dig out."

"What happened after you told him that?"

"He did not like my words, so he departed."

"Had the peyote cleared from his mind by that time?"

"No. He staggered away. The peyote makes a long visit. Its power disappears gradually, but its effects remain throughout most of the next day."

"I guess we can conclude that Broken Wing found his way to Mollie Day's quarters after he left the peyote lodge."

"Yes. I do not know what happened there. But Broken Wing is a peaceful brave, who came of age after the Kwahadi came to this place. He had learned some of the American talk from you as a boy, often spoke with the soldiers. He talked of joining the bluecoats. He thought he might be welcomed by the buffalo soldiers. He had spoken with the lieutenant, Flipper, about this."

Lieutenant Henry Flipper, the first Negro graduate from West Point, was an officer with the Tenth Cavalry buffalo soldiers stationed temporarily at Fort Sill. She knew and liked the young officer and mentally added him to her contact list.

"Broken Wing was a good pupil, and he joined the students at the Methodist school and learned to read and write. I thought he became a Christian."

"The preacher dunked him in the creek, but others of the Peyote Religion travel the Jesus trail, too. A man cannot have too many religions."

Jael, born Jewish and learning the Torah's word until she was fourteen and then shifting with ease to the more informal Comanche religious practices of multiple spirits and deities, ducked the theological debate. "I have a single question. Are you asking me to represent Broken Wing?"

"Yes, I wish you to do this?"

"Who is paying for this?"

"Your fees will be paid from my personal money in the Santa Fe banks. Tribal funds will not be used for defending Broken Wing."

"You have a personal interest in his case?"

"I wish you to keep any mention of the Peyote Religion away from this case. The white men do not approve of the peyote. Bad Hand Mackenzie has told me that peyote worship must stop. The white holy men and the chiefs in Washington believe peyote is evil. If anyone claims peyote caused the woman's death, there will be new attempts to destroy the religion."

"Bad Hand" was the Comanche name often applied to Mackenzie, referring to a misshapen hand and mutilated fingers resulting from Civil War injuries. "I cannot promise this. If you wish to pay for defending Broken Wing, it must be without conditions. He would be my client, and I would be accountable to him alone."

Quanah's grim expression did not change, but his eyes narrowed. "Then I will not pay."

"I will speak with Broken Wing. Do you object if I choose to help him anyway?"

He was silent for some moments before he spoke. "Do what you will."

She started to get up, but he stopped her, speaking English now. "Must talk wives."

"Your wives?"

"Mackenzie say Jesus men no like more wives. Say me should keep one. Tell others go away. Want all Comanche man have one woman. Not Comanche way."

"How many wives do you have?"

"Me have three womans. Soon four."

"The preachers and the government might not bother you so much, if you just keep the wives you have."

"Me want ten wives. Big chief should have most wives. Build big house like white man. Every woman have room."

"This will cause trouble."

"She Who Speaks will find answer for this. Me and you talk this many sunrises." He raised both hands, spreading his fingers.

Ten days. He would get billed for this new headache.

Chapter 4

JAEL TRIED TO locate Michael, whose friends still called him Flying Crow, on the reservation, but his best friend, Turkey Chaser, informed her the boy had headed home. She was not surprised. A condition for reservation visits was arrival at the house by the six o'clock suppertime. Michael refused to carry a timepiece to the reservation, worrying his friends would tease him about turning white, but he had quickly converted Comanche time to the white man's clock in his head.

When she returned home, she found Michael in his father's office reading *The Adventures of Huckleberry Finn*, the novel that had been published by Mark Twain just a few years earlier. He was fond of Rabbit and preferred to remain in the office portion of the structure if his parents were not home. The boy with rust-colored hair and green-flecked brown eyes mirrored Josh not only in appearance but personality. Quiet, reserved, and not given to spontaneity. She found their similarities curious since he had only had a significant relationship with his birth father for a bit over three years, having been taken before his first birthday in a raid that killed his birth mother. This was fine, she figured. She was spontaneous enough for both.

Michael was ensconced in his father's chair so Jael sat down on the chair on the client's side of the desk. "Michael, are you going to speak to your mother?"

He looked up from the book. "Oh, hi, Mom. I love this book."

"This has to be the third time you've read it."

"Fourth. I only have about a dozen books here. I'll probably read it four more times before we go back to Santa Fe. But I can't wait to go to Spiegelbergs and buy every book Mark Twain has written. I'm saving all the money I get from running messages out to the reservation. Next year, I'll bring a wagonload of books back here with me."

The Army employed Michael on a per message basis to deliver requests and information to Quanah and other Comanche contacts because he was fluent in both Comanche and English. His Spanish, with her instruction, improved weekly, and opportunities to use the language in Santa Fe would allow him to hone his conversational skills. If he chose to spend his adult life in the Southwest, his mastering the Spanish tongue would serve him well.

"We do need to upgrade our library here. I will write Rylee. She has promised to catch a stagecoach and come for a visit in August. Perhaps she can bring books along."

"Ask her to see what they have in stock for Mark Twain."

"I can do that. How was your day at the reservation? I saw Turkey Chaser."

"We raced ponies today, but Turkey Chaser won all the races. Some of the others got tired of it and left so Turkey Chaser and I ended up fishing in the creek. We didn't catch anything. Did you hear about Broken Wing?"

"What about Broken Wing?"

"The soldiers arrested him. They say he killed a white lady. Nobody can believe it. He is trying to go the way of the white man. He is very kind. I cannot believe it, either."

"I will have to learn more about this. Now, I need to see about supper. Do you want to come with me or stay here?"

"I'll stay till Rabbit leaves. Wasn't Dad coming back today?"

"That was his guess. It could be several more days, though."

"I miss him."

"Me, too."

Chapter 5

JAEL LAY NAKED on the bed in the second-floor bedroom, only partially covered by a bedsheet. The open window let in barely enough air to justify its use. But she would not have slept even if the night had been cool and balmy. She missed Josh, and if he were here beside her, he would have distracted her from her worries for a fair amount of time. Without her husband as a distraction, she could not turn her thoughts from the tasks on her legal table.

Polygamy among the Comanche and other tribes would not end by edict. How could the Army police cohabitation? Of course, Quanah Parker, because of his high public profile, would be a prime target. It would be hopeless to attempt to force monogamy upon the Indians if the principal chief of the Comanche were permitted to thumb his nose at the rules. General Mackenzie had warned her upon their spring return from Santa Fe that the plural marriages were concerns in Washington but more so among the local clergy and that she should be prepared to deal with it.

Jael had done some initial research at that time and studied the Morrill Anti-Bigamy Act passed by Congress in 1862, which prohibited bigamy in the territories. The legislation was aimed at Mormons in Utah Territory, but from her reading, she had deduced that the law was only nominally effective.

In earlier times she could have claimed the Comanche constituted an independent nation, but the Indian Appropriations Act of 1871 ended United States recognition of the Indian tribes as independent nations. Thus, the anti-bigamy law arguably applied to the Comanche and other tribes. This legislation was also relevant to Broken Wing's status, she thought. The act made it a federal crime to commit murder and other specified crimes within any territory, presumably including Indian Territory. Interestingly, bigamy and polygamy were not specifically recited in this legislation.

The legal conflict between tribal and federal government jurisdictions descended into a quagmire of uncertainty. The reservation system, she figured, assured lawyers of a livelihood sorting out the mess for at least several generations, perhaps in perpetuity. The law firm had ordained her the expert in Indian affairs, but she had so much to learn. Her baptism would come in the morning when she met with Broken Wing.

Enough, she needed her rest. She closed her eyes, willed her worries to retreat, and fell promptly to sleep. Four hours later she awoke abruptly at the sound of a horse blowing softly beneath her open window. She did not bother to rise. She listened. Two horses plodding past the house toward the stable. The creak of leather and tack and then whinnying of the other horses as Josh led his buckskin gelding, Chief, and the packhorse into the stable.

She cursed his dallying in the stable, although she understood his attentiveness to the horses. Finally, she heard his booted feet approaching the house. He would, of course, remove the boots on the veranda, stupidly thinking he could enter the house and creep up the stairs without awakening her. Soon she heard each step of his stockinged feet on the stairway to the second floor. Idiot. Had he forgotten she is Comanche?

She feigned sleep when he entered the bedroom, tugging the sheet over her shoulder and burrowing her head into the pillow but leaving one eye open so she could watch as he undressed. She savored the smell of sweat and leather and horse that wafted her way as he shed his garments, and she thrilled at the sight of his lean, sinewy form, as he stood naked in the moonlight that sifted through the window. He tiptoed toward the bed, and she remained still until he slipped beneath the sheets. When he had settled in beside her, she tossed back the sheet and pounced upon him like a panther, smothering him with hungry kisses, raking and stroking his body with deft fingers.

"Jael," Josh said, "you scared the hell out of me. I thought you were asleep."

His voice was cut short when her lips covered his mouth. She lifted her face from his for just a moment. "You can talk another time. Now shut up and do your duty."

He obeyed.

Chapter 6

JOSH DID NOT stir when Jael slipped out of bed. Poor man. She watched him, his breathing deep and rhythmic in slumber, oblivious to the sweat-soaked sheets upon which he was sprawled. She knew he had pushed himself and his horses to get home and been near exhaustion before she let him take a break from lovemaking. She, on the other hand, received a surge of energy from her husband's return and was anxious to move on with her day. It was not quite six o'clock, and a glowing ember portending the crawling flame of sunrise was just starting to appear on the eastern horizon. She wrapped a light cotton blanket about her body for modesty's sake in case the early-rising Michael should be up and about and snatched a pale-blue dress and some undergarments from the closet and headed downstairs.

The sweet smell of cinnamon biscuits struck when she reached the bottom of the stairway, signaling that Rosa was working her magic in the kitchen. Rosa Fuentez, a plump, middle-aged Mexican woman, was a godsend. She worked three days weekly for the Rivers household, cooking meals, house-cleaning and steaming and brushing clothing items that required special care. An organized, efficient woman with a seemingly perpetual, perfect smile, she prepared food ahead for her off-days and left instructions and ingredients out for those items that could not be preserved.

Josh had found Rosa several years earlier and persuaded Jael that she could not handle all the domestic duties and give proper attention to her law firm responsibilities. She protested at first but now took the assistance as her due. She had travelled some distance from her life among the Comanche.

When she entered the kitchen, Jael was greeted by the smile and a cheery "Good morning, Señora. Coffee is brewing, and a kettle of water is boiling for your bath."

"Good morning, Rosa. You spoil me."

"My pleasure, Señora. Take your bath, and I will have breakfast when you are finished."

A claw-footed tub was in a closet-sized room behind a curtain off the kitchen. Jael had pumped three buckets of water and left them next to the tub the previous evening so they could warm during the night, but the addition of the hot water would be nice. She felt she stunk like a billy goat, although she hated to wash away the smell of her man. She dropped her blanket and retrieved the kettle and poured the hot water in the tub, following it with the water from the buckets. She let herself into the tub and tugged the curtain shut, and she and Rosa gossiped about life on the post while she bathed. They spoke English because neither Rosa nor her husband, Benito, were fluent in the tongue of their more remote ancestors, having descended most recently from several generations of Texans.

Rosa said, "Benito told me this morning you will be the lawyer for the Comanche who killed Mollie Day."

So much for secrets at Fort Sill, Indian Territory. Benito was a leather craftsman, a contract civilian, who employed several others to handle saddle and equipment repairs and restoration at the post. He did not miss much of the fort's news and passed it on to Rosa. "Benito probably knows more about this than I do. I haven't even met with the accused. And remember, a man who has been accused is innocent until proven otherwise."

"So I have heard," Rosa replied, doubt reflected in her tone. "But this Comanche, they say he was found in her bedroom. It seems very strange that an Indian would be there unless he was up to no good."

Jael did not remind Rosa that she thought of herself as Indian, admitting she did not fit the stereotype or, for that matter, the blood lineage. "Did you know Mollie Day?"

"I saw her sometimes on wash days. She was always very friendly and seemed nice."

Jael sensed a thought unexpressed. "But?"

Jael was on her knees in the tub now, scooping water with a cup to rinse her lathered hair. The curtain opened, and Rosa handed her a tin filled with clean, warm water to finish the rinse.

"But," Rosa replied, "some of the women did not like her. They said she was a slut and that others should keep an eye on their husbands when she was near."

"Why would they say that?"

"She was young and pretty, almost as pretty as you. That's enough to make women jealous on an Army post. Of course, they don't worry about you. Why would you want another woman's man when you share the bed of the handsome Señor Rivers?"

After last night, why indeed? "Thanks, I think."

Jael got out of the tub and dried off, pulling the plug to allow the bathwater to drain out a pipe to a nearby gully chosen by Oliver Wolf. The Cherokee promised a remodel soon where he would bring water to the house. He could not yet promise a water closet to replace the outdoor privy, but he said he was considering logistics of such construction. After her life among the Comanche, she still suffered some guilt when she sat on the stool in the water closet Oliver had installed at the residence in the hills outside Santa Fe. All these unbelievable modern conveniences were unnatural and likely destructive to one's character. But she had no desire to return to the days of squatting on the ground in the bushes surrounded by the pungent odors and scattered piles of human waste.

She dressed quickly and sat down to Rosa's breakfast of hot cinnamon biscuits with butter and bacon and a steaming cup of hot coffee. Momentarily, Michael stumbled into the kitchen and sat down beside her and said, "Dad's back?"

"Yes. He returned during the night."

"I thought so. You woke me up."

Oh God. "What do you mean?"

"You were screaming."

"No. You must have been dreaming."

"But they sounded like happy screams. Like when a warrior has taken a scalp."

Jael hastily finished her coffee and stood up. "Eat your breakfast. Let your father sleep. I'm going to step over to the office for a bit and then I must visit a prospective client."

"Broken Wing?"

"Perhaps."

"Can I tell Dad?"

"Yes. Tell him to ask Rabbit about the case."

Chapter 7

JAEL HITCHED THE carriage to a bay mare and drove it the two miles to the Fort Sill guardhouse. She would have preferred a horseback trip, but her long skirt made that prohibitive, and she supposed the soldier guards might see her as more authoritative if she arrived via buggy. The fort buildings were constructed around a large rectangular parade ground, rows of enlisted men's barracks at one end and married officers' houses at the other. Unmarried officers resided in smaller buildings to the rear of the houses, usually providing private quarters with a small bedroom and parlor.

Sergeants and other enlisted officers resided in smaller houses and barracks-type structures along each side of the parade grounds. Stables, trading posts, a hospital and other facilities extended beyond the various living quarters. The guardhouse stood alone beyond the other structures, edged by seemingly endless, dry prairie.

Jael tugged the reins, bringing the carriage to a gentle halt near the hitching post in front of the square-shaped, stone guardhouse. She noticed two soldiers with rifles standing at ease on each side of the entry door, which could be reached only by climbing the eight to ten steps to the railed porch. She grabbed her large, leather shoulder bag, which doubled as a briefcase, and walked with deliberation toward the porch. The soldiers remained in position, but she noticed their curious eyes fixed upon her as she approached the porch and started up the stairs. When she reached the porch floor, she announced, "Privates, I am Jael Rivers. I am an attorney, and I am here to visit one of your prisoners, a young man known as Broken Wing."

One of the soldiers, a lean baby-faced young man, looked at his comrade, a husky man in his mid-thirties with a twisted nose that suggested a few barroom fights. Jael pegged him as a former sergeant who had likely been busted more than once. He was clearly in charge here.

"I know who you are, ma'am. I'm Private Connell. This here's Private Gable. I'm sorry to tell you the prisoner ain't allowed visitors."

Private Connell sounded like he was speaking with sand in his throat, and Jael didn't think he seemed very sorry. "I am his lawyer," she said firmly, realizing it was a small lie until Broken Wing formally hired her. "And I intend to visit him. He is entitled to see his lawyer."

"We got our orders, ma'am. No visitors."

"I would like to speak with your immediate superior. In the meantime, I am going to sit down on the step here until this matter is resolved." She backed away, spread her skirt and sat down on the top step.

"Keep an eye on her," Connell told Private Gable, "I'll talk with the corporal." The heavy door creaked open, and Connell disappeared inside.

More than ten minutes passed before Connell returned with a diminutive, red-haired soldier with corporal's stripes on the sleeve of his blue coat. Jael stood and faced him. She guessed he was not much older than Private Gable.

"I'm Corporal Hunt, ma'am. What seems to be the problem?"

"I explained to Private Connell. I am here to visit my client, Broken Wing. I don't wish to make a fuss. But I will not be leaving until I speak with him. If you don't have authority to make this decision, I suggest you find someone who does. I know my friend, General Mackenzie, would not approve this obstruction of my client's rights."

The name-dropping got the corporal's attention. "Well, ma'am, I do have authority to make exceptions to policy. There is no need to make an unnecessary incident out of this. I guess you can have five minutes with the Comanche."

"I'm sure I will require more than five minutes, Corporal, but the general will be made aware of your cooperation. Now, may I see my client?"

The corporal replied, "Step inside, ma'am. I'll need to check your bag. No exceptions to that rule. Private Gable, come with us."

The corporal's battered desk sat in a little nook just inside the entryway. As directed, Jael dumped the contents of her leather bag, including her derringer and razor-sharp scalping knife, on the desktop. Gesturing toward the weapons, Corporal Hunt asked, "Lawyer's tools?"

"Occasionally."

"You can pick them up at the desk when you leave."

The corporal and Private Gable escorted Jael down a long hallway to the far end of the building. She noted that the cells were all separated by stone partitions with the doors constructed of iron bars that permitted observation of the occupants. Most cells had cots for two occupants, but there appeared to be only three soldier residents this morning, and each was lodged in his own cell. Broken Wing was quartered in a corner cell with a single cot and a large crock jar, which Jael assumed served as a chamber pot. From the odor emanating from the cave-like room, she assumed the pot's contents had not been emptied recently.

Broken Wing, shirtless and wearing faded denims, sat on his cot staring at the wall, seemingly unaware of his visitors. He was a handsome young man, she thought, slim and sinewy, perfectly-carved aquiline facial features and black hair trimmed short white-man style. A full-blood, decreasingly common among Comanche these days, his flawless skin gleamed like polished walnut in the filtered sun rays that creeped though the narrow, barred cell window and illuminated his face. She recalled him being of medium height but seeming taller because of his erect, confident bearing.

"Hey, Comanch," the corporal snapped. "You got a visitor."

Broken Wing seemed not to hear and continued staring at the wall.

Jael said, "If you will unlock the cell door and give us privacy, I will speak with him."

"That's not going to happen, ma'am. I'm not locking you up in there with a woman killer. Something happens to you and the general hangs my balls on the flagpole . . . pardon the expression."

"Perhaps, you can provide me with a chair, and I will sit here in the hallway and chat with him."

"Private, get the lady a chair," the corporal ordered.

The private hurried back down the hallway and entered an empty cell. He retrieved a rickety-looking chair and returned and placed it next to the cell door. The corporal said, "Now you get back if he gets too close. You can see my desk at the other end of the hall. I'll be watching, and you just holler if there's trouble. Mind you, don't be long."

"No longer than necessary," Jael replied noncommittally.

Chapter 8

JAEL SAT IN the wobbly chair outside Broken Wing's cell, remaining silent for several minutes while the soldiers walked to the other end of the building. She was still uncomfortable that the corporal's desk was within easy hearing distance, but that was easily remedied.

"Broken Wing," she said, speaking Comanche, "it is She Who Speaks. I have come to help you. Do you hear me?"

"I hear you," he said, turning his head toward her and speaking English, "I cannot be helped. I am ready to die."

"We must talk about this," she said, again speaking Comanche. "And you must speak only the language of The People. There are big ears in this place."

"I chose the white road. But I will do as you ask. I know you mean no harm. I trust She Who Speaks, who first taught me the white man's words." This time he spoke Comanche.

"Do you understand that I am a lawyer and that it is my job to help persons who are accused of breaking the law?"

"I know this. But if I killed the Great Spirit's guide, I should be put to death also."

"You do not know if you killed her?"

"The soldiers say I killed my guide. I was told I sat naked on the floor of her room when they found me there. I was singing, a soldier said. I do not remember this. It may have been the death chant. Mollie, my guide, was dead, lying in her bed. The soldiers showed her to me, but it is all a fog. I remember nothing but the scarlet lake of blood she lay in."

"I know about the peyote meeting. You were there before you went to Mollie Day's room. Did something happen there to cause you to go to Mollie Day's quarters in the enlisted officer's units?"

"I am not certain I am to speak of the Peyote Religion."

"I have attended a meeting. I know the ceremonies that take place there. I have spoken with Quanah. He is the one who summoned me to help you."

Broken Wing shifted so he was facing her more directly now. "It was my first time. I follow the white man's trail and the Jesus road, but I believe many religions can be good, and I went to the meeting and brought Jesus with me . . . in my heart . . . so I could keep my connection to The People and understand their religion, too. I would be both Peyote and Christian. Quanah said I could learn to be a cedarman."

"A cedarman?"

"One who sprinkles sagebrush incense on the fire and recites special words as he does so. An important part of the ritual."

"I see. But that night you partook of the peyote?"

"Yes, and, at first, I became very ill and vomited many times. Later, though I came to know great peace and joy. There is a white man's word that describes this."

"Euphoria?" she asked.

"Yes. No Comanche word can describe it. Euphoria. I think it is a room in the Jesus heaven."

"And you had a vision?"

"Oh, yes. The Great Spirit told me that Mollie had been sent to guide me in the ways of the white man. That she would be my woman. My only wife, since we would follow the Jesus road together, and Jesus wanted us to have a single mate throughout our lives. This I already believed."

"Did you know Mollie Day already?"

"Yes. We were to become husband and wife under the white man's laws."

"Didn't you know she already had a husband?"

"Not a true husband chosen by the Great Spirit. She was not married to this Sergeant Day."

Broken Wing was confusing her. "So how did you end up in Mollie Day's bedroom?"

"The Great Spirit told me she was in danger. He said a creature of the night planned to kill her and that I should go to her. Then I heard her voice calling for me. So I went to her."

"How did you know where to find her?"

"I had been to her lodge sometimes when the man who claims to be her husband was away."

Jael was incredulous. "You were coupling with this woman before that night?"

"Yes. She said she loved me and that I could lie with her without paying her money."

"Money?"

"I did not understand this. But I think Sergeant Day paid her to copulate. Maybe others, too."

"And you say she told you she was not married to the sergeant?"

"Yes. She said she was waiting for the right man. She told me I was the man. And the peyote spirit told me that I was to be her man, and she would be my guide on the white man's trail. And now that will never be. But Jesus says if I die I will be reunited with her in the white man's heaven. And that is where I want to be. I follow the Jesus road. I do not fear death."

"But what if you did not kill Mollie? What if it was not your fault?"

"It does not matter. I want to go to her."

"Will you let me be your lawyer?"

"I do not need a lawyer to help me die."

"Do you think Jesus or your peyote spirit would wish you to value your life so lightly?"

Broken Wing turned silent. She sensed that he was thinking. She hoped the human instinct for survival was reaching him.

Finally, he spoke. "I must think on this. If you become my lawyer, can I make you go away whenever I wish?"

"A client may terminate a lawyer whenever he wishes, and the lawyer is bound to honor that decision."

"But lawyers are paid to do whatever they do. What must I pay you for this?"

"What do you have?"

"I have a ten-dollar gold piece, some garments at my tipi and eleven horses."

"I will handle your case for my choice of three horses."

"You shall be my lawyer, and if I die you may have the ten-dollar gold piece and all my horses."

"No. No. That is not how it works. That would be very unethical."

"It is time for you to go now. I must think about this. You go ahead and do what lawyers do."

"I shall. In the meantime, you should answer no questions from anyone. Tell them you must talk to your lawyer first. When I meet with you, we will continue to speak Comanche. If I must get word to you, I will send Rabbit with a message, and you may speak freely with her . . . in Comanche. Use English in this place only when you have a request or are responding to something not related to your case. Understand?"

Broken Wing nodded affirmatively with a grave look on his face.

Chapter 9

JAEL PICKED UP her knife and derringer at the corporal's desk, receiving only a few unfriendly grunts from the corporal. She suspected he was annoyed because of aborted eavesdropping during her conversation with his prisoner. When she reached her carriage, she caught a glimpse of movement behind the corner of what appeared to be a small storage structure about twenty paces off the side of the guardhouse. Probably nothing. But she was not unmindful that Broken Wing's case carried a wagonload of unanswered questions as well as serious legal and political implications. Administrators in the Department of Interior and its Kiowa-Comanche Agency would be greatly troubled by prospects of a Comanche being tried and put to death by the United States Army.

This raised an issue she would discuss with Josh. What court held jurisdiction over the case? Military tribunal? United States District Court? There was no federal district court in Indian Territory. She would be waging war on a murky battlefield.

She drove the carriage to a long narrow water trough constructed of a rocky concrete mix on the edge of the parade ground. A private tended the adjacent pump to keep the water source full for horses. She paused to allow the mare to drink and plucked a tin cup from under the seat and climbed out of the buggy to retrieve water for herself. The soldier nodded and worked the pump handle to provide her with a refreshing drink. She drank eagerly and held her cup out for a refill. The ruddy-complexioned, boy-warrior smiled and obliged. She thanked him, but when she turned away to return to the carriage she noticed a mounted soldier on the opposite side of the parade ground who appeared to be showing undue interest in her. She didn't give it much thought. She was accustomed to male stares, especially on an Army post suffering a severe female shortage. Usually, she had to admit, she was flattered by the furtive looks, but, occasionally, she found herself annoyed by the blatantly lecherous stares.

On the dusty trail that led back to the office-residence, Jael tossed a look over her shoulder and was concerned to see a rider following her some distance back. From the shoulders-forward way the rider sat in the saddle, she surmised it was the man she saw at the parade ground. She chided herself for not bringing her Winchester and vowed not to repeat the mistake. She considered giving the bay slack on the reins and making a race for home, but, if the rider wanted to catch up to her, she knew it would be futile to try to outrace him.

She looked back again to see the rider had set his mount into full gallop and her carriage was the obvious target. She started slowly reining in the gelding and reached into her bag, her fingers closing on the derringer's butt.

A high-pitched voice that could have belonged to either sex called, as the rider closed in, "Mrs. Rivers, hold up. I mean no harm. I carry a message."

She brought the carriage to a full stop but did not release her grip on the gun. The rider came up beside her, and she saw a uniformed boy with straw-colored hair who looked like no more than a sixteen-year old, tall and gangly, a scarecrow draped in Army blues. It seemed like half of the soldiers on the post were mere boys, she thought. He certainly did not give her a sense of fierce intimidation, but she remained prepared to respond to any threat.

"You have a message, Private?"

"I can't tell you her name, but a lady asked me to give you this." He tugged an envelope from his coat pocket and nearly stretched free from his saddle as he leaned over and handed it to her. "She said no one was to see me pass this to you. That's why I waited until you left the post."

"Thank you . . . I guess. What's your name, Private?"

"Private Reuben Schultz, ma'am. Most call me, 'Rube.'"

"Reuben, tell your mysterious sender that your mission has been accomplished."

"Yes, ma'am." He pivoted his horse, and, in a few moments, disappeared in a swirling cloud of dust.

Jael opened the envelope and slipped out a sheet of fine parchment inscribed with penmanship that would have won the praise of any teacher. She read the brief message: "I was Mollie Day's friend. There are things you should know about her. Meet me behind the west side of the north stable immediately after sundown."

Chapter 10

JAEL HAD NARROWLY missed noon dinner, but Rosa quickly heated up the beef and vegetable stew and served two slices of fresh-baked bread. She also produced a small jar of honey, which she knew Jael loved with bread or biscuits. A cake that smelled of sweet maple tempted Jael, but she decided to defer till supper, hoping that Josh and Michael would not attack it again before then.

As she washed dishes, Rosa chattered and brought Jael up to date on her family. "Josh got up not long after you left with the carriage. He looked very tired, but his mood was cheerful. Michael was so happy to see his father. A soldier was here very early with messages for him to deliver to the reservation. That is where he is now. He has a very good business."

"Yes, he does. And he's very careful with his money. Whenever we see Rylee, he gives most of his earnings to her to invest at the bank." Jael shifted subjects. "Is Josh in his office?"

"Yes. He told me to tell you that he would be there when you got back. I told him about the killing of the sergeant's wife, and he seemed very concerned."

Jael got up from the table and took her dishes and silverware to the kettle of water that Rosa had boiled for washing. "I'd better bring Josh up to date. When Michael gets back, would you tell him to check with us in the office?"

When she entered the office, Jael found Rabbit leaning on an oak filing cabinet next to Josh's door. "Is Josh meeting with a client?"

Rabbit started and turned toward Jael before moving quickly to her desk. "Not exactly. General Mackenzie stopped by."

"A general does not just stop by a lawyer's office. Especially, when the lawyers do not represent the government."

"I never eavesdrop, of course, but I happened to be up getting a file from the cabinet next to Josh's door."

"So, what are they talking about?"

"The general says there is going to be an Army trial for Broken Wing and that Rivers and Sinclair will not be permitted to represent him. A captain has been appointed as his lawyer. He does not want any trouble from the firm over this. He says the incident could be very messy, and certain things should not be said at the trial."

"What things?"

"Peyote. This would not be a good thing, he says. It could upset people in Washington."

Jael smiled. "You forgot to get the file. You went back to your desk empty-handed."

Rabbit shrugged. "I'll get it later."

"Well, I'll go in my office. I don't wish to speak with the general. I'll let Josh tell me the story. Let him know I'm here when the general leaves." She entered her office and gently closed the door behind her.

She sat down at her desk and plucked the strange note from her bag and laid it out on the desktop. She had already concluded a woman had written it. Reuben Schutz said a lady had given him the note, and the handwriting was clearly feminine. But that did not guarantee it was not written at a male's instructions.

There was a tap on the door before it opened. Josh stepped in, a grim look on his face. Jael stood up and stepped around the desk, giving him a lingering kiss on the lips.

"Cheer up, lover. After last night, you should have a smile on your face." She gave him a peck on the cheek and returned to her chair as he pulled up a chair opposite hers and sat down. This husband of hers tended to be too serious, but his closed lips surrendered a small sheepish smile.

"So General Mackenzie paid a visit?" Jael asked.

"If you know that, Rabbit probably told you the entire story."

"No, I came in too soon and spoiled her investigation."

"Investigation? I think the word is snooping."

"I gather the general does not want me to represent Broken Wing."

"That is correct. His trial will be in front of a military tribunal. No civilians involved. That's according to Mackenzie."

"I don't think the general can dictate that. The Northern Army conducted tribunals and put Indians to death for siding with the Confederacy during the war. Courts subsequently found the Army had no authority to do this. The presiding officers were court-martialed and discharged or demoted. I will call this to the general's attention, and I do not think he will want to take that course without the defendant's consent."

"Tell me what you know," Josh said.

She started with her summons from Quanah, explaining the chief's concerns about the Peyote Religion's involvement. Then she told him about her conversation with Broken Wing at the guardhouse.

"So, do you think he's innocent?"

"I have no facts upon which to draw a conclusion. But does it matter? You have always said it is not our job to determine guilt or innocence. The defendant is entitled to a lawyer's best efforts. Also, I do believe that our client does not know if he killed Mollie Day or not."

"Strong evidence that he did."

"Entirely circumstantial. Easily a reasonable doubt. I will urge our client to plead not guilty in whatever court we appear."

"You keep saying 'our client' and 'we.' You've already decided you're going to represent him, haven't you? Remember, you are still an associate. You must have the law firm's approval to accept a controversial case."

"I sleep with the senior partner. He's a good man. I can't imagine he would not approve."

"Is Quanah going to pay for this?"

"No. Not unless I promise to keep peyote out of it. And I cannot promise that."

"It sounds like he and the general are on the same page. Who's going to pay your fees?"

"First, Danna assured me the firm will take on worthy cases without charge from time to time. Second, I have agreed to a three-horse fee. I intend to take Rabbit with me to select the horses from Broken Wing's small herd soon."

"Three horses won't go far on a case like this."

"Better than nothing. And I did not want to leave him destitute."

"We'll be destitute if you keep taking cases like this. Why am I not involved in picking the horses?"

"You have a pile of work on your desk and don't have time. Besides, you would just pick the pretty ones. They aren't necessarily the best."

"I picked you, didn't I?"

"Your taste in women far exceeds your taste in horses. And, perhaps, you weren't the one who did the choosing. I do know a fine stallion when I see one." She winked and smiled, knowing she had disarmed him. "Now, take a look at this."

She slid the note across her desk, and Josh picked it up. He looked at her after he read the message. "What do you make of it?"

"Information somebody's afraid to divulge publicly? Perhaps someone is going to give me my reasonable doubt."

"Cases don't get solved that easily. Maybe it's a set-up."

"To get me? Why? I received this note from a young soldier . . . Private Reuben Schultz. If something happened to me, it would be a simple matter to track the chain of delivery back to the source."

"I know this is a stupid question. Are you planning to meet with this person tonight?"

"Of course."

"I can follow you and be there to back you up, just in case."

"I don't think that's wise. You would probably scare the person off if you were seen. You can help, though."

"You tell me how."

"Loan me your Army Colt."

"Done. Now would you like to hear about some legal business that will make the firm some money?"

"Certainly."

"I negotiated a deal with Charlie Goodnight at his Palo Duro Canyon operations. Next spring he will deliver two hundred bred heifers and cows to the reservation for Quanah to establish a foundation for his own herds. He will also drive a thousand head of his own to graze on Comanche grassland at one and a half times the highest lease rate Quanah is getting this year. Charlie's advice will come free, and he will help Quanah get started in the cattle business and furnish some competition for the leased land. Local ranchers will have to up what they're paying if they don't want out-of-territory cattlemen out-bidding for grazing rights. Two wins for Quanah."

"That's wonderful, Josh. Quanah will be pleased." She was sincere and happy for her husband's success but thanked the Great Spirit she rarely had to deal with this boring side of the profession.

"I'm having Rabbit help me put together contracts and leases. That will take a week, but I'll ride out to the reservation tomorrow to explain to Quanah what we've worked out. I'm sure he'll go for it."

"I cannot imagine otherwise."

"I would usually want your help when I take him the paperwork. He can't read much English yet, and we don't do very well verbally. Since you have this murder case on your plate, I thought I'd take Michael with me tomorrow to interpret when we hit the rough spots."

"That sounds like an excellent idea. Quanah likes Michael. He wanted to be his father."

"With you as his third wife. Don't remind me. I'm sure he doesn't know what it would have cost him in sleep."

"Poor Josh. You are tired, I know. I was just so happy to have you back."

"Jael, I hope you'll always be happy to have me back. Life with you is an adventure I wouldn't miss for anything. Did I tell you last night I love you?"

"Not that I recall."

"Liar. But I love you anyway."

Chapter 11

Jael, dressed in buckskin britches, sleeveless shirt and doeskin moccasins, sat astride Trouble behind a screen afforded by a grove of cottonwoods near the creekbank a quarter mile from the northernmost buildings on the military post. Her Winchester was cradled in the saddle holster and the Colt and knife tucked in the shoulder bag she would keep with her. The fiery sunset was burning out now, on the brink of disappearing behind rolling hills many miles to the west. As a shroud of darkness dropped onto the plains, she nudged the gelding out of the cover and toward the northeast corner of the Fort Sill compound where one of the enlisted cavalrymen's stables was located.

As she neared, she veered away so she could approach the front of the stable, which faced south. She dismounted and hitched Trouble to a hitching post. She stood quietly and listened for some moments before she stepped softly toward the west side of the building. When she reached the corner she pulled the Army Colt out of her bag and hesitated, and then she quickly made the turn with weapon ready to fire. No one there. That did not concern her. It only meant she was first.

Jael's back hugged the stable's wall while she waited for her rendezvous with the unknown contact. Fifteen minutes passed and no appearance. She had about decided the message sender had succumbed to second thoughts about the invitation when she sensed movement near the northwest corner of the building. She turned her Colt in that direction.

"Mrs. Rivers?" The tentative, female voice came from around the corner.

"Yes. Who is it?"

"I sent the note." A petite woman stepped from behind the corner and walked slowly and uncertainly toward Jael. As she neared, Jael could see that she was young, perhaps, her own age—twenty-five years or so. The darkness did not hide the color of her blonde hair, pulled back in a pony tail. Long skirt, but practical short-sleeved, white blouse. She had seen the attractive woman at the post mercantile. Melinda Carson, a first lieutenant's wife.

Jael moved toward the woman, her hand extended. "I'm Jael."

The visitor hesitated and then responded with a trembling hand damp with perspiration. "I am Melinda Carson, and I may be a fool for meeting you here."

"I doubt that. You obviously have something important to tell me, and when a man's life is at stake I do not think it foolish to shed light on something that might lead us to the truth. And I gather from your note that is what you feel compelled to do."

"I have a question first. Will whatever I tell you be kept in confidence? Can you promise me I will never have to testify in court about our conversation?"

"I cannot promise on either count. I will discuss our conversation with my law partner, who happens to be my husband. I will say nothing to anyone else unless it becomes necessary for the defense of Broken Wing. But if you have information that might save my client's life, I would have you subpoenaed to testify if I had no alternative. Subject to those caveats, I assure you I will try to protect you and that I will not repeat your words frivolously."

Melinda took a deep breath. "I am afraid, but I like your honesty."

"Why are you afraid?"

"My husband. He knows nothing of this. He is very ambitious and, to be honest, something of a priggish sort. We have been married only a bit more than two years, and I love him, but I wish he would be more understanding of others' imperfections. It could be very troublesome for our marriage should he find I have not been entirely forthcoming with him."

"I am intrigued now, but this is your choice. If you do not wish to speak with me, I will leave and not press you further."

For a moment, Melinda looked like a frightened rabbit, and Jael feared she was going to pivot and run. Then she set her jaw firm, and her eyes narrowed. "I cannot live with myself if I don't share what I know. If Andrew learns of this, so be it. I guess he will have to decide what he wants to do about it."

"Your message said Mollie Day was your friend."

"More than that. She was my sister."

The information stunned Jael for a moment, and she recognized she must handle the interview very carefully. No pushing. Let Melinda tell her story. "I see. I can understand how difficult this must be for you."

"She came back from Fort Worth with Colin Day because she knew I was at Fort Sill with Andrew. We grew up in St. Louis. Our father was very strict and a drunk who did not spare the razor strap. I was the eldest of five, and I left home at seventeen and was fortunate to secure a position with a bank. I was able to support myself. I met Andrew when he came in to cash his Army scrip. Mollie was five years younger and was not so fortunate. She ran away at sixteen and ended up in a bordello. Somehow, she found her way to Fort Worth. She had no contact with our parents, but a year after she left I received a letter from her, and after that we corresponded every three or four months. That's how she knew where I was."

"She married Sergeant Day because you were here?"

"She didn't marry Sergeant Day."

"I don't understand."

"She met him at the house where she worked. He was . . . a customer in the bordello. She learned where he was stationed and encouraged him to visit again. After a week of visits, he fell madly in love with her and begged her to marry him. She declined his proposals but said she would return with him to Fort Sill and live with him for a time. He could call her his wife, and when she left, he could claim they were divorcing. The poor sergeant truly loved her, I think, and figured he could eventually convince her to marry him. He treated her like a princess, and she kept her part of the deal by taking care of him in bed and doing the laundry and other domestic chores."

"But this doesn't explain how Broken Wing happened to be at their residence."

"She lived a complicated life here . . . certainly not one I condoned. But she was very forthright with me. She intended to make all the money she could here and then move on to Denver or Santa Fe and open her own house. She was very ambitious. She took in laundry, baked for officers' parties . . . she could have opened a bakery someplace . . . and when her so-called husband was gone . . . which was frequent and for long periods . . . she procured several customers for her . . . uh . . . professional services. She asked me to hold her funds in a special account in my name. There is over a thousand dollars there. She could have left the post with that money. I wish she had."

"Are you saying Broken Wing was one of Mollie's customers?"

"No, no. But he was her lover."

Just when Jael thought Mollie Day's story could not get more bizarre, Melinda came up with another twist. "Let me summarize. Mollie lived with a man under the pretense she was married to him. She serviced other men as a prostitute on the side. And she had a Comanche brave as a lover."

Melinda shrugged. "I guess that sums it up. She suffered no moral conflicts with any of this. She saw it all as a path to a better life, and, if she made others happy along the way, what harm was there to it? That was her outlook. Broken Wing became her problem, however."

"What do you mean?"

"She loved him. Or thought she did."

My God. Where was this leading? "A Comanche brave? That's something that would be frowned upon in white society . . . if not outright taboo."

"But if the sexes were reversed, much less so. Correct?"

"I can't deny that. A man can take an Indian wife with not much more than a lift of an eyebrow." She almost added that she was Comanche married to a white man. That's still how she thought of herself, but she carried not a drop of Comanche blood in her veins. She was, in fact, by birth a German Jew, which some bigots might find worse.

"Well, it happened. She encountered Broken Wing when she was walking near the creek little more than a month ago. They ended up talking for several hours. After that, they met almost daily, at first just to talk, but, of course, one thing led to another and the rendezvous quickly became intimate. He visited her residence a few times when the sergeant was off post. But he was not a customer or client, whatever the proper term is."

"Did she ever speak of violence between them?"

"Just the opposite. She told me of the relationship three or four days before her death. She said he was the kindest, most sensitive man she had ever known. She said she would be needing the money I held for her because in a few weeks they planned to disappear from the post and reservation. They would be married as 'Mr. and Mrs, John Wing.' He would sell his ponies, and they would start a respectable business somewhere. They had it all planned out. She had started declining visits a few days earlier to the annoyance of several of her customers evidently."

"Was she threatened by someone?"

"She didn't say that. She just said several were very unhappy with her. She told me she could understand . . . I'm embarrassed to say this . . . because she was very good at her work. Does that shock you?"

"Be assured that it is nearly impossible to shock me with anything. I have not lived a sheltered life."

"No, I suppose not."

"Do you know the names of any of her customers?"

"No, she said it would be unprofessional to violate their confidence. And I did not wish to know because they were probably officers."

"Why do you say that?"

"Mollie told me she was quite expensive, and the money she turned over to me verified that. An enlisted man would most surely been unable to have afforded her services."

"Is there anything else you can tell me?"

Melinda hesitated. "No. I just want the killer to pay. And if it was Broken Wing, I will gladly watch him face the firing squad. But I do not want an innocent man to die, either. The truth. That's all I want."

Jael was convinced there was more to Melinda's story but decided not to press. They would talk again. "Then you can help in the search for the truth."

"I hope I have done the right thing by coming to you."

"You have done the right thing. And you are a woman of courage. Mollie deserves to have justice done. I intend to find it."

Chapter 12

IT WAS APPROACHING eleven o'clock when Jael returned home. Josh had been pacing the floor, worried half-sick, when he heard her ride in. By the time she put up her horse, entered the house and walked into the parlor, Josh had sunk in his stuffed leather chair next to a kerosene table lamp thumbing through legal documents he had intended to review but had been unable to focus on. He put the sheaf of papers aside and got up to greet her when she came through the door, pulling her gently into his arms and planting a kiss on her forehead.

"It took you a while," Josh commented, not admitting he had been struggling with the urge to ride out and look for her. If it had not been for his reluctance to leave Michael alone, he would have been on his way an hour earlier.

"I had an interesting evening. But I was never in danger."

"You look tired. Why don't we get ready for bed, and we can talk about it there . . . if you want to. I admit I'm curious."

"What if I don't feel like talking?"

"Your choice. You'll think of something."

Later, as they lay in bed, savoring a rare cool breeze that drifted through the window, carrying what could turn out to be a false promise of rain, Jael cradled her head on Josh's shoulder, tossed her arm over his chest and a leg over his thigh. The press of her flesh against his own tested his restraint and self-discipline.

"Why don't you tell me what happened tonight?" he said.

"Really?"

"You're itching to tell me about it."

So she told him every detail of her meeting with Melinda Carson. When she finished, she said. "My wildest imagination turned loose could not conjure up a story like this."

"It's beyond strange, I'll give you that. Are you thinking you are representing an innocent client? That would be nice for a change."

"I'm not sure. But, if reasonable doubt is the standard, the door has been opened."

"I've been thinking about this. From my conversation with Mackenzie I suspect the Army is going to be moving forward quickly to put the case before a military tribunal. That means an officer might be appointed to represent Broken Wing. You could be denied the right to represent him."

"But the military has no jurisdiction. This is a civilian defendant."

"We've talked about this. They've done it before."

"But the United States District Court has jurisdiction over the Indian Territory."

"I agree that's what the statutes say, but I don't think we'll find much case law to back it up. There hasn't been time for cases to reach the Supreme Court. Besides, our firm probably has more expertise on the law pertaining to Indian affairs than any lawyers west of the Mississippi, and we don't know all that much. It's very murky stuff. Also, consider that if you are successful in avoiding the tribunal, the case goes to Fort Smith, Arkansas. The District Judge there is Isaac Parker . . . no relation to Quanah, by the way."

"The Hanging Judge."

"Yes. So, pick your poison."

"The witnesses are here. The tactics of trying a case at Fort Smith, Judge Parker notwithstanding, would be a nearly impossible burden. I would rather take our chances at Fort Sill . . . if the Army will let me represent Broken Wing."

"I might be able to help."

"I would welcome any assistance I can get."

"If you like, I'll talk to Mackenzie and suggest that I'm going to summon Tabby to report on the case if the Army refuses to allow the firm to represent Broken Wing. She would love to get hold of a story like this. And the military hates bad publicity."

Tabitha Rivers was an independent correspondent for the Santa Fe Daily New Mexican and a best-selling author of a fiction work titled The Last Hunt, based roughly on the lives of Jael and Josh. She had also authored a non-fiction book, Dismal Trail, which chronicled the Kwahadi perspective of the final months that ended with Quanah leading his people to the reservation. She had a base of fans hungry to read her stories and the ability to ignite a political thunderstorm over mistreatment of the Indians. She had her share of detractors, but the commandant at Fort Sill would no doubt prefer to avoid the attention of press and public to any tribunal, especially one that might be conducted under dubious authority.

Jael said, "Why don't you do that? I suspect the general worries I am too close to Quanah. Of course, what you are proposing borders on extortion."

"No, it doesn't. Just gentle persuasion. I also know a few sergeants who might, with a few drinks under their belts, share some gossip about the love lives of their superior officers. If you want to know what's really happening in the Army, Pop always said to ask a sergeant. He knows where the bodies are buried."

"Do you really think you might learn something from one of the sergeants?"

"We have nothing to lose. Cavalry Sergeant Timothy Clancy's about to call it quits, and he's an old friend of Pop's. They served together under then Major General Zachary Taylor in the American-Mexican War over thirty years ago. If anybody knows anything, Tim will. Or he will know who does."

"You can be useful sometimes," she mumbled before her eyes closed and she dropped off to sleep.

Josh smiled and kissed the top of her head before he joined her.

Chapter 13

GENERAL MACKENZIE PROMISED to issue an order authorizing the Rivers and Sinclair firm to represent Broken Wing in the trial before the military tribunal conditional upon the attorneys refraining from any objections to the tribunal's jurisdiction over the case. During their meeting in the general's office, Mackenzie demonstrated that he knew how to play the game as well. He was obviously a step ahead of the lawyers when it came to the political and legal implications of the trial, and Josh had not been forced to play his publicity card, at least not openly. Ranald Slidell Mackenzie knew Tabitha Rivers personally and by reputation and was certainly not oblivious to the fact she and Josh were siblings.

Josh also learned that the tribunal would convene in approximately two weeks and would consist of five officers, including Major Abraham Stone who would preside. Mackenzie provided a list of the other tribunal members, consisting of a captain and three first lieutenants. The name that leaped from the handwritten list was First Lieutenant Andrew Carson, doubtless Melinda Carson's husband. Another bear trap to tiptoe around.

Josh was headed now for the northeastern edge of the military post toward a tract of what had been dubbed 'no man's land,' a desolate patch of about ten acres claimed by neither the military nor the reservation. The unclaimed property was the location of active civilian commerce, however, that included a trading post and tavern with log storefronts and mostly canvas-covered frames for walls and roofs. The floors consisted of rust-red, fine dirt. Behind the more permanent structures, a tent city thrived among a mix of discarded Army canvas wall tents, some tipis and no small number of two-person, wedge-shaped abodes that had been dubbed "pup tents" during the Civil War. The latter were used mostly as sleeping quarters for the entrepreneurs and their employees. A row of the pup tents set off from the others were occupied by prostitutes for their business transactions.

Josh easily found the building with a scrap-wood sign tacked above a blanket-covered doorway that proclaimed the enterprise "Big Bo's Retreat." He pushed the filthy blanket aside and entered, finding himself immediately struck by the suffocating heat. He loosened his shirt collar and removed his string tie, thankful he had left his coat at the stable with his horse after visiting the general.

There were not more than a dozen customers in a canvas-covered cavern that would hold well over a hundred, and he quickly spotted the beefy, white-haired soldier. He was hunched over a rickety table near one wall, where someone had rolled up the canvas a few feet to allow some air to sneak in. Josh walked over to an old work bench that served as a bar and ordered a sarsaparilla for himself and a mug of beer to deliver to Sergeant Timothy Clancy. Thus armed, he strolled over to the sergeant's table and sat down.

The sergeant looked up and blinked his eyes. "Lordy, son, I thought I was seeing my old pard, Levi Rivers. You're his spitting image from thirty-odd years back."

Josh shoved the beer in front of Clancy, who pushed aside his empty mug without comment. "The beer's hot, the sarsaparilla's hot, and this place is a sweat lodge. They call it a retreat. From what?"

"From the Army, son. No self-respecting commissioned officers would set foot in this place, and that's good enough for me."

"When I saw you a few months back, you said you'd be out before the end of July. You didn't re-enlist, did you?"

"Nope. Time to go. Can't hardly climb on a damned horse anymore. Problem is I don't know nothing but Army. And even if my pension finds its way to me, it ain't enough for a man to eat on, let alone drink a proper amount. Don't know where I'm going or what I'm going to do."

"I told you last time we talked that Pop wants you to go out and see him. He always needs help on the Slash R."

"I never worked cows, and I don't want charity."

"And Pop won't give charity. You'd have to earn your keep. He needs someone who can be in charge . . . handle other men. That's what you've done most of your career."

"I suppose I could go for a visit just to talk about old times."

"Do that and see what happens. Pop would love to see you."

Clancy straightened up a bit, swiped his shirt sleeve across his forehead, ruffling his white, bushy eyebrows and then cocked his head to one side and stared at Josh with piercing pale-blue eyes. "A man who is married to the purtiest woman in all the southwest and wears fancy duds and drinks pig piss . . . this don't seem a likely place for him to spend his leisure time. Why would I think it ain't accidental you came to be sitting at this table?"

Josh smiled, took a swig of warm sarsaparilla and winced. Maybe it is pig piss, he thought. "I won't deny it. I had hoped to find you here. I was trying to track you down and an unnamed private suggested I might look here. I confess to ulterior motives, but I swear that what I said about Pop was fact."

Clancy chugged his beer down. "Get me another, and then we'll talk."

After Josh retrieved the beer and sat down again, the old soldier said, "Tell me what this is about."

"Mollie Day's murder. Jael is representing the young Comanche man who's charged with killing her."

"Did he do it?"

"That's for the military tribunal to decide."

"I think they call them weasel words. But I don't see what this has got to do with me."

"Did you know Mollie Day?"

"Yep. I'd guess about everybody knew Mollie. Most liked her. Pretty as a little red heifer in a flower bed. Sweet as fresh apple pie. Spoke to everybody. Even grumpy old men like me."

"Did you know anybody that did not like her?"

"Some of the women folks didn't. Jealous maybe. Afraid she'd catch a husband's wandering eye."

"Enough to kill her?"

"I couldn't say. How much do you know about the little lady?"

Josh knew he had to be careful here, divulging just enough, perhaps, to trigger a flow of information. "I've picked up rumors that Mollie may have had a secret life, that she may have seen men besides her husband."

"Is that so?"

"You don't seem surprised."

"There have been stories. But I never held it against her. None of my business. Besides Colin Day was old enough to be her father and one unpleasant bastard to be around . . . has a cruel streak. Clubbed Comanche women and babies to death with his rifle butt and smiled when he did it. Decent men give him a wide berth."

"I'm trying to find out who the other men were. Any ideas?"

"Maybe. But these things generally stay with the Army."

"When an innocent man's life is at stake?"

"I don't know that he's innocent. And he's Comanche."

"My wife is Comanche. My son was raised Comanche."

"Meant no offense. But they're not blood. That's different."

Josh did not have time to debate the grizzled sergeant. "Regardless, we can't learn the truth without the facts."

"What the hell. You're Levi Rivers's boy. And I'm out of uniform in a few weeks. Mollie had three officer friends I heard about. Captain Milo Crawford, Lieutenant Grayson Downs and Lieutenant Andrew Carson. I'm sure there's another one or two I ain't heard rumors of. Somebody said when Day was out on patrol, several would call on her the same night . . . different times, of course. Strange goings-on. I don't know what was happening. Don't want to."

Carson again. Mollie's brother-in-law. Did he know Mollie was his wife's sister? Did his wife know her husband was one of her sister's clients? And he was a judge on the tribunal. Where was this leading? Josh thought about reviewing the list of tribunal officers with the old sergeant but thought better of it. Perhaps another time. "Can you tell me anything about these three men?"

"Haven't served under them. Captain's said to be a good officer. Taskmaster. Goes by the book sort of officer. But a fair man. Heard Downs comes from money . .

. lots of it. His old man's some kind of senator back east. West Pointer. So's Carson. Snake. Cold as a banker's heart. That's all I'm going to say."

Chapter 14

JAEL STEPPED ONTO the boardwalk outside the post infirmary on her way to visit with the senior post surgeon, Captain Charles Olson. She had met the physician on several occasions. A tall, blond man with Nordic features and complexion, she was certain most women found him handsome, as did she. But there was a distance and aloofness about him that made her uncertain how to best approach him. Businesslike and straightforward, she decided. No small talk or personal chatter.

When she entered the hospital, Jael found her eyes burning slightly from chemical fumes that also stung her nose. She cast her eyes about the cramped hospital ward and noted there were no more than half dozen patients in the beds that lined the walls on each side of an open corridor that divided the long room. To her left, she got a glimpse through several open doorways of long, white tables, and she assumed these rooms were the surgeries. She surmised that the three rooms to her right were private offices or examination rooms.

She saw a young soldier, covered with what looked like a butcher's apron, walking down the corridor in her direction. As he drew nearer, she was surprised to find that she knew him—the scarecrow messenger, Private Reuben Schultz.

"Howdy, Mrs. Rivers," he said, sheepishly as he walked up to her. "Pleasure to see you again."

"Private Schultz, I didn't expect to find you here. But it's nice to see you, too. You work here, I gather."

"Yes, ma'am, I'm an orderly officially, but more of a jack-of-all-trades. Some days, I'm a nurse. Today, I'm a janitor. I've been scrubbing the floors and walls with buckets of water mixed with a carbolic acid solution. That's what you smell. Captain Olson is worse than my mom when it comes to keeping things clean. No criticism intended, ma'am. The captain ranks up there with God in my book."

"Perhaps you can help me then. I would like to speak with the captain."

"Sure, that's his office," the private said, nodding to a room with a closed door. "I'll check with him. We're not too busy right now. No war, and we're long removed from winter, when we're always filled up. We just got a few slackers and dysenteries to deal with so far today."

Private Schultz went to the office door and knocked. He was admitted and shortly returned, followed by the captain, who was immaculately attired in his dress blues, looking more like an attendee at an officer's ball than a working physician this morning.

The captain tendered just the slightest bow and said, "Ma'am, Private Schultz says that you would like to speak with me. How may I be of assistance?"

"I am the lawyer for the young Comanche man, Broken Wing. I understand that you were called to examine Mollie Day's body after her death. I would like to speak with you about her injuries and see if you have other information to share that might shed light on what happened that night."

The captain hesitated for a moment, obviously sharing the uneasiness many folks had when it came to answering questions from snoopy lawyers. Peacetime Army promotions came very slowly, and she guessed that promotions were never far from this man's mind.

He would not want to jeopardize his place in line by saying the wrong thing.

He nodded to the private, who lingered nearby. "Private, you're dismissed." Turning back to Jael, he said. "We can talk in my office."

Olson led her into his office and seated her at his polished, oak desk, which bore ornate carvings and was clearly a piece of furniture far above Army quality, obviously provided from personal funds. As if reading her mind, he commented, "The desk is a gift from my wife, who unfortunately has been unable to join me at this posting."

"Captain, I know that you are a busy man, so I will move directly to my questions. I would like to confirm the cause of Mollie Day's death. You did examine Mollie, is that correct?"

"Yes, I most certainly did."

"Where did this take place? Her residence or at the infirmary?"

"I was summoned to the married enlisted men's quarters in the middle of the night. I examined her body on the bed."

"Was Broken Wing there when you arrived?"

"No."

"Can you describe what you found?"

"I feel like I'm a courtroom witness."

"Consider this a rehearsal."

"I don't want any part of a controversy."

"I'm sorry, Captain, you already are. But if you just state the facts, there is no reason you should undergo any unpleasantness. You are just a soldier performing his duty. Tell me, who called you to the quarters?"

He shook his head doubtfully. "A private whose name I don't recall. He was on guard duty and had walked by the quarters and heard an eerie chanting coming from inside. He tapped on the door and when he got no reply, opened the door . . . which was slightly ajar . . . and, through the open bedroom door, saw a naked Indian sitting at the foot of the bed. He called for the corporal-of-the-guard, and he and a lieutenant came to assist."

"Were you at the infirmary when you were summoned?"

"Yes, I had volunteered for the night duty to relieve one of the surgeons whose wife had been a bit under the weather." He nodded to a cot situated along the wall to her right. "It is not unusual for me to spend the night here. Anyway, I rushed to Mollie Day's quarters, but the instant I stepped into the room, I knew she was dead. She had bled out, and the blankets were blood-soaked.

Some of the blood at the edges of the quilt was beginning to crust and dry."

"Was anyone else there when you arrived?"

"A corporal and the private who had summoned me. And there was a first lieutenant."

"Do you know the lieutenant's name?"

"Oh, yes. We occasionally join some other officers for an evening of poker . . . no serious stakes, mind you. Lieutenant Carson. Andy Carson."

Melinda Carson's husband. Mollie's brother-in-law, although the lieutenant was unaware of it. Or was he? Jael said, "How did the lieutenant happen to be there?"

"I have no idea. I suppose he was called out by someone in authority to supervise the handling of the incident. He said he had ordered the killer . . . that's what he called the Comanche . . . to be arrested and delivered to the guardhouse."

"Did you see a weapon anyplace?"

"No."

"Tell me about Mollie Day. You found her on the bed?"

"Yes. She was obviously killed there. Other than droplets on the floor and a bedside rug, the blood was confined to the bed. The killing was a bit overdone. She was stabbed multiple times. She was stabbed once in the chest and twice in the stomach. Any of these would have killed her. There were other shallow wounds, and then her face was crisscrossed with slices. Looked like a grizzly bear had worked her over. She also incurred cuts on her wrists and arms, quite obviously resulting from attempts to defend herself. I hate knife wounds. Messy stuff. I'll take a simple bullet wound any day. Better way to die, too, I'd think."

"Why would anyone mutilate her this way? They had to be very angry."

"Or crazy. Or in a drunken stupor."

She could have done without those observations. "What kind of knife likely did the damage?"

"Big one. Body thrusts went as deep as I've seen. Might have been a butcher knife."

Captain Olson seemed thorough enough, but she had an uneasy feeling she was not asking him the right questions. He made her a bit uneasy the way he looked at her with a steady gaze and undressed her with his eyes. But he was quite handsome in his dress blues.

Chapter 15

JAEL AND JOSH sat in sturdy rocking chairs that had been crafted by their friend, Oliver Wolf, who also designed the roofed veranda that had been added the previous year and stretched the length of the stone house. Josh had a booted foot propped upon the porch railing as he rocked slowly, gazing dreamily out into the star-spangled sky that was like a giant lantern that lit up the prairie. Jael's rocker was motionless, and her mood was pensive, evidenced by her silence and her chewing of her lower lip, which Josh knew she was prone to do when something worried her.

"So what do you think?" Jael asked

"About what?"

"Broken Wing's case. What else?"

"I don't think Danna is going to be pleased about a three-horse fee for all the time we're putting into this."

"You are the senior partner. I would think you could decide your own fees."

"I didn't decide, remember. You negotiated terms with the client. And Danna manages the firm's finances. I earn three times what I made before she signed on."

"She can fire me if she's unhappy with my billings."

"Can I still sleep with you?"

"Joshua, I am attempting to communicate about case strategy."

Joshua. The signal her patience was being tried. But she was so beautiful when she was pissed. Josh said, "I think one of us needs to speak with Lieutenant Andrew Carson. His name keeps turning up at very inconvenient places. At the least, you are going to have to call him as a witness. We can't allow him to take a seat on the tribunal under those circumstances. You must either file a motion to have him removed as a hearing officer, or we have to convince him it would be prudent for him to withdraw because of a potential conflict of interest."

"You are right. I should speak with him soon."

"I was hoping you would allow me to approach him."

"Why?"

"First, you need to spend some time with your client. And then you should start your trial preparation. I don't know if we have anything in our library about procedure at military tribunals, but I suggest you humble yourself and ask Mackenzie to assign an experienced officer to the case to assist with military issues. I understand the defense counsel would have been a Captain Markham if we had not intervened. Perhaps he could be assigned as co-counsel to the case."

"I don't like the idea. He might try to take over the case. He's probably annoyed that we stepped in anyway. We don't need to work with a hostile partner."

"Just a suggestion."

"I'll think about it."

"A military tribunal is foreign territory. A guide might keep us off the wrong trail."

"Like I said, I'll give this some thought."

"It's your case. Anyway, I would still like to deal with Lieutenant Carson. I think it would be less compromising for you where you have already spoken with his wife."

"That makes a certain sense, I guess. Go ahead, if you wish."

"I'm taking Michael with me to visit Quanah about the Goodnight contracts in the morning. Knowing Quanah, that will probably eat up most of my day. But I'll track

Carson down the next day and find out what he's got to say."

Jael reached her hand out and grasped Josh's, giving it a squeeze before clasping it firmly. "Thanks," she said, "for being my friend, among other things."

"What are the other things?"

"Later."

Chapter 16

J AEL WALKED DOWN the guardhouse hallway unescorted this time. When she reached Broken Wing's cell, she peered in and froze. His body dangled from the end of a rope hitched to a rafter, his legs kicking spasmodically and his feet no more than a foot from the stone floor's surface. His fingers clutched and dug frantically at the loop that burrowed into the flesh about his neck.

Jael screamed, "Corporal. Emergency. Prisoner dying."

The corporal at the desk got up and began to stroll casually down the hallway, until Jael yelled again. "Get your ass moving, Corporal. This man dies and you face a court martial."

This got the guard's attention, and he began running, unclipping the keyring from his belt as he raced toward Jael. By the time he reached her, Broken Wing's arms had dropped to his side, and his head drooped forward. The guard fumbled with the keys and finally swung the door open. Jael burst through the opening, bent to wrap her arms around the young Comanche's legs and lifted with all the strength she could muster, hoping to cause enough slack to ease the rope's death grip. Meanwhile, the corporal stood on the cot from which Broken Wing had launched his suicide attempt and sawed at the suspended rope with his penknife.

When the rope split, the young man's body collapsed on Jael and drove her to the floor. She pushed him off and scrambled to his side, clawing at the rope that still clung to his neck like a strangling collar. Finally, it began to loosen, but she feared it was too late. She pulled the rope away, and Broken Wing's head flopped lifelessly against her thigh. Bile rose in her throat, and she struggled to keep from sobbing.

Then, a cough and the slightest movement of his head. Another cough and the fluttering of his eyes. She shifted her position on the floor so the young man's head could rest on her lap. She caressed his face softly with her fingertips. "Corporal," she said in a voice barely above a whisper. "Water, please."

"Yes, ma'am."

The soldier raced down the hall like a general had issued a directive and returned quickly with a canteen and handed it to Jael. "My bag," she said. "There is a handkerchief in it. Just reach in and find it."

The corporal complied. "Ma'am, there's a gun in the bag."

She took the handkerchief and began to drip some of the canteen water on it. "Yes, it's a Navy Colt. You forgot to check my bag when I came in. But I won't tell anyone if you won't."

"Uh, no, ma'am. I won't say a word. Thank you, ma'am."

Jael brushed the moist cloth gently over the young Comanche's soft cheeks. He coughed some more and started to lift his head and shift his body. The corporal knelt and helped Jael scoot Broken Wing to a sitting position, leaning against the cot. He appeared dazed and confused, but he would survive this foolishness, she thought. Now she felt less pity than anger for one who would abandon the gift of life so easily. She could not grasp the notion of such surrender to the hardships and challenges of fate. These were things to be dealt with and overcome. She had watched her parents undergo brutal and tortured deaths at the hands of Comanche who later became her new family. Not for a moment had she considered anything but survival.

Jael turned to the soldier. "Corporal, where did this rope come from. Do you furnish your prisoners with suicide ropes?"

The corporal's face reddened. "No, ma'am. Never. I don't know where this came from."

"Well, please remove it from the cell. And I'm going to bring my chair in from the hallway and talk to Broken Wing in here. Any objections?"

"No, ma'am. Whatever suits you."

She pressed the mouth of the canteen to Broken Wing's lips. He clasped it with shaky fingers and swallowed, coughed up the water, and then sipped.

Chapter 17

"YOU WILL LISTEN to me, and you will answer my questions. Do you understand?" Jael said, speaking Comanche.

"Yes, She Who Speaks," the young brave replied in his Kwahadi dialect, his voice subdued and contrite.

"Do you know how stupid that was? The Great Spirit gives life only to those who value it. If you had died, you would have wandered alone in darkness for eternity. What you did was not only stupid but an insult to your ancestors and to all the spirits."

Broken Wing sat on the cot, his face glum, staring at the floor. "I tried to stop. I knew I did not want to die the moment I stepped off the cot and kicked it away. I tried to stop, but it was too late. If you had not come here, I would have begun my journey in the darkness."

"You were taking the coward's trail. A warrior fights till his last breath is forced from him. Now, sit up. Lift your head. See my eyes."

A startled look crossed the young Comanche's face, but he straightened his body and shoulders and met her gaze.

"That is better. If you wish to kill yourself, you must tell me. I will bring you another rope, or, perhaps, a knife so you can at least feel the point of the blade and die like a warrior. I will leave now if you wish to run like a hunted rabbit from this battle."

She glared at him with icy, dark eyes. He did not flinch. "I will fight."

"Where did you obtain the rope?"

"Someone left it on the floor while I was sleeping."

Jael looked up at the single, narrow-barred window. Too high for someone to reach from the outside. A person could toss up a rope, but a prisoner would have to be able to grasp it, possibly by standing on the cot since the window was above eye level.

"Why do you think someone might believe you would use a rope to kill yourself?"

"I have not been brave. I have cried for the loss of my Mollie. I have screamed at the guards that I wanted to die. In English I have begged them to kill me. If I killed her, I should die also. And in the white man's religion I would see her again in heaven."

"No, you would not. If you killed her, you sinned, and you will burn in the devil's hell. Now, I want to talk with you again about that night . . . and before. And we continue to speak the language of The People."

"Many things I do not remember. But I will try."

"Who has visited you since I was here."

He was silent and seemed to be searching his mind for answers. "Rabbit. You sent her with questions. Then Lieutenant Carson . . . asking what I remembered of that night."

"Those two. That's all?"

He thought some more. "I believe the doctor came, but I am not certain."

"What do you mean you are not certain?"

"I may have been dreaming this, but I think he gave me medicine to help me sleep. But this may not have happened."

"Is it true that you planned to leave the reservation and marry Mollie . . . start a life in the white man's world?"

"Yes. How did you come to know this?"

"I was told by someone who cared for Mollie."

"Her sister? Melinda, the lieutenant's wife?"

"You know of the sister then?"

"Yes, she tried to help Mollie. I saw her on the post, but we never spoke. Mollie told me she talked to her sister about us and that Melinda cared for her white man's dollars."

"We must talk more about what you remember of the night of Mollie's death, however painful."

"Yes. I know this now. And I must learn what I did that night."

"You told me earlier that when you became one with the peyote spirit, you had a vision that Mollie would lead you into the white man's world. But you had already decided this yourselves. Why did the vision have any meaning to you that night? You had already created your own vision of what your life was to be."

"I see that now. But the peyote spirit also warned me Mollie was in danger and that I must help her. I had forgotten this. That is why I went to her lodge. But I still wonder if I was the danger, the creature of the night who killed her."

"Do you remember more of that night since we last spoke?"

"I think of things, but I do not know what is real or what comes from the peyote or might be a memory of another time."

"Tell me things you have thought of."

"I see myself coupling that night in Mollie's bed. But suddenly I realize she is dead and I see my body rising and floating like a spirit from the bed, and I begin to sing the death song. Sometimes, the more I think on this, the more I become confused."

"Broken Wing, you said you were aware that Melinda Carson knew about you and Mollie. What about her husband, Lieutenant Carson? Do you think he knew?"

"I do not think so. Mollie did not want him to find out. And he said nothing to me."

"Said nothing to you? Are you talking about when he came to see you yesterday?"

"Yes. He came to visit me. He tried to ask me questions about what I remembered of the night Mollie died. Like you. But I remembered you told me not to speak with anyone. I pretended I could not speak English and could not understand him. It made him quite angry. I remembered him from the night at Mollie's lodge. He was there with other soldiers when I awakened. I think he was in charge, but I only remember seeing Mollie and the blood and being taken to the guardhouse. After that, I collapsed again and did not awaken until the sun was at its highest."

"Keep trying to remember. I am going to send Rabbit here to check on you twice daily. If you have anything to tell me, send a message with her." Jael paused. "There is one other matter I must bring up."

"Yes?"

"Our fees. I am going to have to charge you five horses for my services. Your case has become very complicated."

"I own the finest horses. Your fee seems high. But I will pay. Choose your horses when you wish. But I will pay no more horses."

"I will not ask for more."

Chapter 18

It had been Josh's misfortune to catch Quanah Parker in a bad mood this morning. He had not seemed particularly pleased to see his lawyer and, at first, claimed he did not have time to discuss contract matters. When Josh mentioned a great deal of money was involved, but he could come back at a more convenient time, the chief decided he would make time. They were seated now on robes in the tipi where Quanah discussed business matters. Josh would call it a Comanche office, sans desk or furniture. He suspected the first principal chief of the Comanche would remedy that soon enough.

Michael sat at Josh's side opposite the chief in case interpreting services should be required. Josh shuffled through papers in his soft leather briefcase while Quanah looked on with a scowl on his face.

"Womans fight today. Kicks Too Much near bleeding time. Cause trouble then. Others no like anyway. Need new woman. One not cause trouble. Think maybe Prairie Dove. She seem nice. Sixteen, seventeen summers."

Another wife. Sounded to Josh like a good way to start a war. It did give him an opportunity to present a simple legal theory that he had come up with on the ride to the reservation, although he had not had the opportunity to clear it with Jael. "I think I have come up with an answer for the government or the churches if somebody complains about the Comanche having too many wives." Quanah looked at him quizzically, and Josh nudged Michael who repeated his father's words in Comanche.

"Tell me," Quanah replied.

This might work, Josh thought. Quanah can reply in English, but Michael would translate Josh's words. Jael and the chief always had an easy flow of words between them using seemingly bizarre combinations of both tongues. "You marry your women in a Comanche ceremony. These are not registered in a Bible or other white man's records, so they are not recognized as true marriages under white man's law." He nodded for Michael to translate.

Quanah cracked a smile and nodded. "So, Quanah no have any wives under white man law. Cannot have too many womans. Jesus people and Washington go away."

"Probably not. They will complain, but you just say you have no wives. That should keep them confused for a long time. And we can defend you in any courts if they try to do something. I don't think they will for a good while."

Michael translated again.

The chief replied, "You good lawyer. Will pay. Now tell She Who Speaks help Peyote Religion. Pay her monies, too."

"Now, Chief, we must talk about the Goodnight agreements and leases." Josh handed Quanah the documents to look over. "I know you are reading some English now, but I will explain each provision of the leases and agreements. If you wish, Michael . . . Flying Crow . . . will read and translate to Comanche."

"Me look. You talk. Not too much."

First, Josh summarized the documents, emphasizing that Quanah would receive bred cows and an equal number of unbred heifers, along with sufficient bulls to service them. These cattle would provide the foundation for a quality herd. In addition he would collect fifty per cent more rent on any land leased by Goodnight. He spoke slowly as the chief thumbed through papers. He doubted if Quanah was doing much reading, but he was a shrewd, intelligent man who had an amazing comprehension of finances for a man just several years removed from what many whites considered a primitive life. Josh was married to the woman who had counseled the former war chief and was very aware he was no fool.

Quanah passed the papers back. "Me sign now."

Josh plucked a small ink bottle and pen from his briefcase. "Our secretary, Rabbit, typed two identical copies of each contract and lease. You will have to sign your name ten times."

Quanah stood and untied a stiff buffalo-hide war shield from the tipi wall, sat cross-legged and placed it on his lap. Michael scooted next to the chief and held the ink well as Quanah carefully spread out each signature page on the shield and then dipped his pen after printing each letter until he had inscribed 'Quanah Parker' in large, thick letters. Josh, sensing that the process was something of a spiritual moment for the chief, remained silent until every page had been signed.

Quanah broke the silence first. "Now Goodnight do this?"

"Yes, I will employ a rider to deliver this, and he will bring back a copy with Goodnight's signature. Charlie might even come here and bring it with him. He said he would like to meet with you when the deal is made."

Josh realized he was saying too much too fast because Quanah's brow furrowed in confusion. Michael leaped in and interpreted before Josh signaled, however, and Quanah nodded approvingly.

As Josh and Michael walked back to the hitching rack to claim their mounts, his son asked, "Are you going to get more wives, Dad? Quanah is about your age, and he is already looking for a fourth wife. Most Comanche men have at least two wives."

"I'm not Comanche, son. And your mother is wife enough, I promise. Besides, she would make herself a widow if I tried to take another wife."

"I don't understand."

"Never mind, Michael, I was just thinking out loud. By the way, you did a fine job today. The firm will pay you for your work."

Michael grinned. "Easy money. I like that."

Chapter 19

WHEN JOSH AND Michael returned early afternoon from Quanah's tipi compound, they found the carriage in the stable so Josh figured Jael had returned from her guardhouse visit. While he was anxious for her report, his stomach won out, and he entered the house door and made a beeline for the kitchen. Michael, on the other hand, took the office entrance so he could tell his mother about his adventure as a professional interpreter.

Jael was the only mother Michael would ever remember, and Josh would be forever thankful that his infant son's abduction by Comanche took the boy to the woman She Who Speaks. He told Michael from time to time about Cassie, the tough, fair-haired beauty who had given him life, not hiding the truth that Comanche, the people he thought of as his own, had murdered her. But he always skirted the specifics and never dwelt on the heinous crime, deciding his son should take his own time to sort out and come to terms with the messy questions of right and wrong. There was a lot of ambivalence in the moral issues raised by the conflict between the Indian and the white man. Damned if he had worked it all out in his own mind yet. Probably never would.

Josh's nose told him before he reached the kitchen that Rosa had prepared one of her Mexican dishes, and when he walked in she was already placing a steaming plate of bean-stuffed burritos on the table.

"I saw you ride in, and I had saved this back for you and the cub. The dessert, though, is plain old American apple pie. I hope you don't mind my mixing cultures."

"Never. It's always delicious. But you can stay away from the Comanche dishes. I never wanted to know what I was eating when I was visiting a Comanche village."

He ate ravenously and thanked her when she put a steaming tin mug of coffee next to his plate. "You spoil me, Rosa. You're not expected to wait on me like this."

"That's why I do it sometimes . . . because you don't expect it."

"What kind of mood is Jael in? I was curious how her morning went."

"She seemed sad and preoccupied about something. She is never unpleasant, but I can tell when something's troubling her. She will be fine after she talks to you."

Michael walked in with a big grin on his face. "I smell burritos."

"Sit down," Rosa said. "A plate is on the way."

"Is your mom busy?" Josh asked.

"Nah. She's just looking at a bunch of papers. I told her about our visit to Quanah."

Josh was uncertain what the visit was like through a nine-year old's eyes.

Josh got up and took his plate and utensils to the sink. "Well, I'd better get over and tell her my version."

"Yeah," Michael said, "she said to tell you she needs to talk to you."

When Josh walked into the reception area, Rabbit waved him through to Jael's office. Josh set his briefcase on Rabbit's desk. "We've got Quanah's signature on everything. Do you suppose you can figure out the quickest way to get the contract back to Charlie Goodnight? We'll hire a rider if we have to."

"I can already tell you. There will be a stage passing through tomorrow on its way to Santa Fe. The Post mail's going with it, and it stops at that little settlement near

Palo Duro. I'm sure Mister Goodnight gets mail there or somebody will get it to him."

"Makes me nervous, but it's the best we can do short of personal delivery, and I can't take the time off right now. See if you can get it packaged up, and I'll write a note later to send with it."

He walked into Jael's office and took a chair in front of her desk.

She looked up and said, "Your son wanted to know what it meant when you told him I would make myself a widow if you brought home another wife."

"It was a joke. He heard me talk to Quanah about the wife problem and had questions."

She lifted her eyebrows. "I explained to him that his dad was joking and what being a widow meant. He assured me you weren't bringing more wives home. I told him I wasn't worried about it."

"Lord, no. I can barely handle one."

"Michael said Quanah signed the Goodnight contracts. He was quite proud of his part in the visit."

"He should be. He's a fine interpreter. Knew exactly when to break in if the conversation faltered. I promised him payment from the firm, and I'm sure he won't let me forget about it."

"It will free up my time if he can handle some of the translating work for you. Now, tell me about Quanah's wives."

Josh explained his theory that Quanah did not have multiple wives because there had been no attempt to formalize the marriages under American or territorial law. "How could he be prosecuted for bigamy unless the government grants full faith and credit to Comanche laws? That will happen when hell freezes over."

"You are suggesting he is just cohabiting with multiple women?"

"Happens all the time among the whites."

"Congress could pass a law specifically declaring multiple marriages conducted by the Indian nations illegal and bigamous."

"But that has not happened yet, and my guess is that such legislation is some years away. Fornication is not a violation of any civil or criminal law that I'm aware of. We can hold the preachers and military at bay for a good amount of time yet."

Jael frowned and rubbed her chin thoughtfully. "You make it sound too easy."

"Sometimes that's why we don't see the answer. It's so simple we waste our time looking for a complicated solution."

"But it's not a permanent solution."

"Since when is anything permanent? Especially with the maniacs in Washington at work."

"I'm glad to have an excuse to put the wives aside for now. Now, allow me to tell you about my day." She told Josh about Broken Wing's attempted suicide and his revelation that Lieutenant Andrew Carson had visited him at the guardhouse. She also related the details of her visit with the post surgeon, who confirmed Carson's presence at the murder scene. "Strangely," she said, "Captain Olson did not mention his visit to help Broken Wing at the guardhouse."

Josh said, "It's interesting how Carson's name keeps popping up. This has travelled beyond coincidence. I'll confront him tomorrow."

"I am going to visit with Captain Omar Calhoun. General Mackenzie sent word that he will be the prosecuting officer."

"A lawyer?"

"No. But he is no stranger to tribunals. He has had more experience than either of us in that venue."

Chapter 20

LOCATING LIEUTENANT CARSON turned out to be a simple task for Josh. A cherubic-faced second lieutenant, sitting alone in the large, drab roomful of desks shared by the lower-ranking commissioned officers, informed him Carson was presently confined to the post infirmary. He declined to elaborate, teasing Josh's curiosity. That could be easily enough satisfied, he figured.

When he arrived at the infirmary, Josh asked to speak to the senior surgeon, Captain Charles Olson. While he waited for the surgeon, his eyes searched the hospital ward. Two young patients sat on the edges of their beds with a table shoved between them, evidently playing poker and using black and red checkers for currency. They did not appear to be suffering unduly. Then he spotted someone stretched out next to an open window at the far-end of the room. The pale soldier lay motionless, and Josh wondered if he might be dead.

He turned when he heard a nearby door open and footsteps on the wide, cedar planks. A tall, impeccably attired officer approached, and, from Jael's description, Josh guessed he was about to meet Captain Charles Olson.

"Mr. Rivers," the man said, extending his hand and offering a firm grip. "I am Doctor Olson. The orderly said you wish to speak with me?"

"I actually wish to speak with an officer who is apparently a patient here."

"That would be Lieutenant Carson. He's the only officer in the ward."

"Yes, it's important I speak with him."

The surgeon shifted the conversation in a different direction. "I assume this is about Mollie Day's murder. I spoke with your wife about the matter at some length."

"And we both appreciate your cooperation. But now it's critically important that I speak with Lieutenant Carson."

"I'm sorry, but he is in no condition to talk. He was in great pain. I put him in a peyote coma."

"Peyote?"

"Very effective. When our laudanum supplies run short, I often prescribe peyote. Have the patient chew the buttons or mash them up and dissolve in coffee. Sometimes more helpful than laudanum."

"But it's not a medication."

"If it accomplishes a medical purpose, it's a medication."

"Where do you obtain it?"

"I have an enterprising Comanche friend, whose name shall remain undisclosed, who is adapting very quickly to capitalism. He provides a consistent supply. I am writing a paper for a medical journal on the subject. Laudanum is an opiate derivative and can be very addictive. Peyote seems much less so."

"May I ask the nature of Lieutenant Carson's problem?"

Olson hesitated. "It's not my practice to discuss a patient's ailments with unauthorized parties, but this is a military post. There are really no secrets here. He has a nasty cut along his rib cage. I've treated it and stitched it. It's not life-threatening unless it putrefies . . . which is always a risk with such things."

"A cut? How did that happen?"

"He says he stumbled in the kitchen and fell on a butcher knife he was slicing meat with."

"You sound doubtful."

"Anything's possible. But it took some acrobatics for a man holding a knife to fall and accidentally drive it into his own ribs with a downward slice. Think about it."

Josh pondered the mechanics of such a maneuver. "It does seem unlikely. But why is he lying?"

"That's beyond my expertise. You're the law wrangler. You figure it out."

"My I speak with him and see if he is able to respond?"

"You can try. He's probably lucid beneath the peyote fog. But he hasn't been very talkative." He gestured toward the man in the bed at the far end of the room. "Help yourself."

Josh walked down the corridor that ran between the rows of empty beds. Lieutenant Andrew Carson appeared oblivious to his approach and did not even turn his head when Josh took a chair beside the bed. "Lieutenant Carson," he said, "I would like to speak with you for a few moments, if I may."

The young officer turned his direction, wincing for a moment as he shifted. Despite his stubbled cheeks and drawn face, Josh guessed many females would find his translucent-blue eyes beguiling. "Who are you?" He asked with a raspy voice.

"My name is Josh Rivers. I'm a lawyer. My firm is representing a young Comanche man accused of killing Mollie Day."

"I can't speak with you. I'm a member of the tribunal."

"That's why you should speak with me. I'm giving you an opportunity to recuse yourself before I present a motion to disqualify before the entire tribunal." Josh could see he had captured the officer's attention now.

"Why would you do that?"

"I've compiled quite a list. First, you were present the night of the murder. Evidently, one of the first two or three persons on the scene. We intend to call you as a witness. You can't act as both judge and witness in a case."

Carson's face paled at the mention of appearing as a witness. "I know nothing about what happened there."

"That remains to be seen. But you were the senior officer involved in Broken Wing's arrest. Since that time, you have visited him at the guardhouse, and somebody left a rope in his cell and planted the suggestion he kill himself. He almost succeeded. We consider you a suspect."

"That's ridiculous. Why in the hell would I do that?"

"An easy way to put the case to bed. And the victim was your sister-in-law."

A flash of panic crossed the lieutenant's face. "How did you know that?"

"That's not important. But when that is revealed to the tribunal, I am confident the presiding officer will promptly order you removed. You should consider saving yourself the embarrassment."

Carson's shoulders sagged in resignation. "I will withdraw if you promise not to disclose my family relationship with Mollie."

"I can't promise that. If it is important to the defense of our client, we'll do what we must. Frankly, I don't care if you withdraw or not. You will not be sitting on the tribunal. That's a promise I can make."

Carson sighed heavily. "I will withdraw. Now get the hell out of here."

"Not before I have asked a few more questions. How did you happen to be one of the first to arrive at the murder scene?"

"I was having difficulty sleeping and I was strolling the parade grounds when I heard someone shout for the corporal-of-the-guards. I followed the sound of the voice."

"What did you find when you arrived at Mrs. Day's quarters?"

"The Indian was sitting naked on the floor, tossing his head about, chanting some gibberish. Mollie was on the bed. Her body and the bed covers were a bloody mess. I checked to see if she was alive. She wasn't. I sent the guard who found her to find a post surgeon, although I knew it was hopeless."

"Had you been sleeping with Mollie?"

Carson's head jerked back, and his eyes sparked with anger. "How dare you suggest that, you shyster bastard? Get out of here now. I have nothing else to say to you."

Chapter 21

JAEL SAW JOSH in his office when she returned from her visit with Captain Omar Calhoun, but he was staring pensively out his window and didn't appear to notice her presence. She looked at Rabbit, who just shrugged and rolled her eyes and then decided not to disturb him and entered her own adjacent office. She sat down and shuffled through the papers Rabbit had placed on her desk, but her mind was not processing the words. It was focused on Broken Wing's case.

She looked up when she sensed Rabbit's presence in the doorway. "Yes, Rabbit?"

"I did like you asked this morning. I went to the guardhouse to visit Broken Wing. The guards gave me no trouble."

"They received orders to be generous with visitors from our office."

"He was surprised to see me there . . . and he remembered me."

"You carried a message to him a few days ago and you are both Kwahadi. He should remember you."

"Yes, but he never seemed to see me in the village."

"You are both older. You are a woman now . . . and a very pretty one. He would have to be dead not to see you. How was he today?"

"He feels very foolish about trying to kill himself. He is sad, but I saw the desire to live in his eyes. I think he will be okay if you permit me to visit frequently."

"I suspect you have an ulterior motive, but, yes, you should see him as often as possible. Did he speak of Mollie Day's murder?"

"That is why I came in. He wanted me to tell you something."

"Well, don't keep me in suspense."

"The night of the murder, when he was crossing the parade grounds toward the non-commissioned officers' housing, he remembers seeing someone coming from the direction of Mollie's quarters . . . a woman. At the time, he thought she was a spirit . . . he says he saw many spirits that night . . . but now he thinks this woman was not. She was going in the direction of the officers' housing but suddenly vanished from his sight."

"Could he make out her face?"

"No, it was hidden by the darkness and a bonnet. She moved quickly and wore a flowing dress and had a slim waist and womanly form. Men." She shook her head in feigned disgust. "Even in his peyote stupor, he noticed her body."

Jael smiled, "Yes, they can be so blind about important things and so keen-sighted about others. Of course, I recall that you had made a rather lewd remark about Broken Wing's form a few days back. Is it possible that women are not so blind about such things, either?"

Rabbit blushed, "Perhaps I should return to work."

"Speak with Broken Wing again. Try to gently help him recall what he can of the night of the murder. The sighting of the woman may be significant. He may remember other things that could help save his life."

"Female talk? Or can I join the party?"

Rabbit started and turned her head toward Josh who stood behind her just outside the doorway. "I was just telling Jael about my visit with Broken Wing, but she is all yours now." Rabbit ducked past Josh and returned to her desk.

Josh entered Jael's office and sat down. "Ladies first," he said. "Tell me what you've learned."

"Oh, I'm a lady now? That might have been the first time you've called me a lady."

"I can't believe that. I know for a fact you're a woman. I've seen you with your clothes off a time or two. And I've watched you behave like a lady when in polite company."

"That's enough of your charm. But now we're on Rivers and Sinclair time. I did meet with Captain Omar Calhoun. He, incidentally, is a true southern gentleman. He's slightly on the portly side with thick hair that is white as snow and a soothing baritone voice that I could listen to all day. Even though he has no formal legal training, he looks and talks more like a lawyer than you do."

"And what do I look and talk like?"

"A rancher. You are most certainly your father's son."

"Should I be worried about this man?"

"Only if you don't get serious about this case."

"Okay, I'm listening."

"Captain Calhoun, despite his lawyerly manner and appearance, is not anxious to try this case before the tribunal. He is an infantry officer and a very intelligent man. He is very aware of the political sensitivity of any trial and the fact that the tribunal's jurisdiction is tenuous at best. Our objective should be to convince him that there is a good deal more than reasonable doubt about Broken Wing's guilt. If we can do that, he will move for dismissal. I have not told him anything about what we have discovered to this point, but he has promised he would sit down with me and listen to any evidence and my argument."

"Any man who saw you would promise you that."

She ignored his remark. "I judge him to be an honorable man. But we need a plausible alternative to Broken Wing's guilt. Rabbit told me something our client has recalled about the night Mollie was murdered."

"You've got my full attention."

Jael told him about the woman the young Comanche had seen crossing the parade ground.

"And you have a theory about the identity of the woman?"

"I don't know that it is theory yet, but Melinda Carson was convinced Broken Wing had not killed her sister. If she was the spirit woman and observed him that night, she knew her sister, Mollie, was dead before his arrival."

"That's true enough. It also places Melinda Carson on the suspect list."

"You're suggesting Melinda killed her own sister?"

"Only the possibility. I've seen some damn tough women in these parts, not excluding present company."

"That doesn't make sense. Melinda was helping Mollie save money for a new life. She had formed a fresh bond with her here at Fort Sill. And I could see she was visibly distraught at her sister's death."

"What if she learned her husband was on Mollie's patron list? Could that have ignited a rage that would have driven her to do something like that? I am not saying she did, but can we really remove her from consideration?"

"I suppose not, but it's hard for me to see her as a violent person."

"Lieutenant Carson is in the infirmary with a knife wound. Claims it was an accident. Captain Olson, the senior post surgeon, is skeptical. So am I."

"You think his wife did it?"

"Why else would he hide the identity of an assailant?"

"I think I should interview Melinda Carson again."

"If you do, watch out. She may be deranged."

Chapter 22

JAEL HITCHED HER carriage horse on the rail near the parade grounds and walked deliberately along officers' row toward the Carson residence. The morning sun glared in her eyes as she moved along the dusty path. She stopped and turned when she heard the low growl of thunder in the west. In the distance she could see the dark, rolling thunderheads moving toward Fort Sill. Probably another false alarm, she supposed. Such clouds had teased the surrounding prairie at least twice the past few months, offering up only bolts of dry lightning and leaving a few scant sprinkles for the parched grasslands in their wake.

She rapped on the Carsons' door and, momentarily, a pallid-looking Melinda Carson appeared. A flash of fear crossed her face when she saw Jael, and she started to shut the door. Jael blocked the heavy cedar door with her foot, however, and shoved it back, thrusting Melinda Carson backward and causing her to stumble before she regained her footing.

"I must speak with you, Melinda. Now," Jael said, her voice soft but firm.

"I have nothing to say."

"Would you rather talk to me on the witness stand at the tribunal?"

Her eyes widened like a frightened doe's. "No. No. I couldn't bear the public humiliation."

"May I sit down?"

"I . . . I guess so." She gestured to a settee at the far end of the parlor in front of a small window which afforded some light in the dusky room,

Jael closed the door and took a seat next to Melinda on the firm sofa. The young woman looked down at her trembling hands where fingers twisted and intertwined nervously.

Jael spoke softly and without emotion. "I am going to ask you some questions. If you wish me to stop, tell me, and I will leave. Do you understand?"

Melinda nodded. "Yes."

"You told me you were certain that Broken Wing did not kill Mollie, but you did not tell me everything you knew, did you?"

"No."

"You saw Broken Wing that night, didn't you?"

"Yes. I saw Broken Wing staggering toward Mollie's quarters as I was leaving. Mollie was already dead."

"Did you kill her?"

Melinda's eyes widened in horror. "Me? Why would you ask that? You can't believe I would murder my own sister."

"I have seen much violent death. I believe anyone might kill if confronted with certain circumstances. I have killed those who have threatened me or those I love. And I would do it again."

"I loved Mollie and was thrilled when we were reunited here. But I suddenly came to hate her."

"What happened?"

"She seduced Andrew. He became one of her so-called customers. I learned a few days before her death when he was late one evening, and I went for a stroll along the parade grounds and saw him leaving the Day quarters."

Jael was not surprised given Lieutenant Andrew Carson's involvement at so many points in the narrative and considering what Josh had been told by his old sergeant friend. "Did you hate her enough to kill her?"

Melinda looked horrified. "No. Never. She was still my sister. I just wanted her to leave Fort Sill with Broken Wing as soon as possible. And I confronted her and told her that the morning she was murdered."

"And what was her reply?"

"She was very emotional. She sobbed and said she was sorry. She begged me to forgive her. She told me that a month earlier Andrew had found records of the money I was holding for her and told her she would never see the money if she didn't submit to him. He was having his way with both of us during this time. It's humiliating to even think about it."

"Then he knew you and Mollie were sisters?"

"He had suspected because Mollie and I became such fast friends and apparently looked somewhat alike. As I look back, I remember he often asked about our relationship and if we knew each other from somewhere before Fort Sill. I shouldn't have lied to him. It was all so complicated and depraved. And I was her conspirator in the tawdry business."

Jael said, "I gather Mollie promised to leave?"

"Yes, I said I would give her a draft for the balance in her account and three hundred dollars cash I had held back. They could use the cash to get started on their journey and open a bank account with the draft when they arrived at their destination. She promised she would be gone within a week. Sergeant Day was expected to return within a week, and she would inform him of her plans. His patrol just rode in yesterday, and he was given the news about the woman he claimed was his wife."

"Josh or I must speak with him."

"She told me she had a man who was being difficult about her terminating her services. She had promised to speak with him that evening, and after that, she would start preparations to depart."

"But you went to visit her again?"

"Yes. I went to tell her I loved her and forgave her. Of course, I still resented the relationship, but I did not want us to part with bitterness between us. I know firsthand how manipulative Andrew can be. And I have suspected he has been with other women when the opportunity arose. He is what some call a tomcat. I refuse to endure it any longer, and I am finished protecting him. I will be leaving the post soon and will divorce him. Perhaps your firm can help me with the legalities."

"That depends on how this all plays out. Tell me more about what you found when you visited Mollie that night."

"She didn't answer my knock on the door, and my first thought was that that she had been persuaded by the unhappy client to relent for a final time. But the curtains were open, which did not seem consistent with that, and I peered in and could see the glow of the kerosene lamp through the open bedroom door. I rapped on the door again and then entered the parlor and called out her name. I just sensed something wasn't right. I walked slowly to the bedroom, calling out for her again. Of course, that's when I found her lying naked in a lake of blood on her bed. I will never forget her twisted face and horror-stricken eyes. The picture is carved in my memory."

"And she had been stabbed?"

"Many times. But her throat had been cut, also, very precisely from ear to ear."

This was the first Jael had heard of the throat wound. That seemed less like a crime born of rage. A wound of that sort would seem to require more deliberation. Why would a killer make a stabbing attack and then cut the throat? It seemed more likely to Jael that the sequence would be reversed. For that matter, it was strange that both types of killing and maiming wounds should appear. Ordinarily, would it not be stab or slice? This new information baffled her.

Jael asked, "When was Mollie buried?"

"The day after her death. The post has no embalmer. And Colin Day's patrol was far south tracking Comanche who had jumped the reservation. They could not delay, so the chief surgeon, with General Mackenzie's approval, authorized burial."

"Why didn't you notify someone of Mollie's death immediately?"

"I panicked. I didn't know how to explain my presence. And I wasn't prepared to place my husband in jeopardy. I needed time to think it all out. By the time I resolved to notify the guards, the body and Broken Wing had already been discovered."

"Will you testify before the tribunal, if necessary, about what you have told me."

Tears streamed down Melinda's cheeks. "Yes. I will not let Broken Wing die for something he did not do."

"I will arrange for the two of us to meet with the prosecuting officer, and he may move to dismiss the charges."

Melinda sighed deeply. "I would be so grateful for that."

"Your husband is in the infirmary with a stab wound. It was not an accident, was it?"

"In better light you would see that my cheek is bruised and swollen. We quarreled after I confronted him about what he was doing with my sister. I accused him of killing her, and he struck me and called me a whore. He said all women are just whores. I lost my head and grabbed a knife from the table and drove it into him. I could not believe what I had done. I opened the door and screamed for help. When soldiers rushed in, he lied and told them he had fallen on the knife. At first, I thought it was such a noble thing to do. Later, I realized he had no choice if he wanted to avoid a full inquiry into the circumstances."

"Do you think Andrew killed Mollie?"

"He denies it, and I cannot quite believe he did. Why? I already knew of their sordid arrangement. She was leaving the post. I was the only other person who was aware . . . as far as I know. My pride would have kept me quiet, and I'm certain he was confident of that. The situation likely would have ended our marriage, although Andrew no doubt believed he could charm me back to his bed." She paused. "And, perhaps, he would have. I confess that I struggle with a devil perched on my shoulder when it comes to intimacies with Andrew."

Jael held back a smile at the notion that lust equated evil. She was thankful that her Comanche upbringing had left her with no such inhibitions when it came to Josh. She hoped this young woman would someday find a mate with a man worthy of her passion.

Jael said, "I believe what you have told me, and I will setup an appointment with Captain Omar Calhoun, who has been assigned prosecution of the case."

"But I won't know any true peace until we know if Andrew is the murderer."

"Nor will I. And I cannot clear the doubt about Broken Wing's guilt in many minds until we confirm the identity of the real killer."

Chapter 23

JOSH WAS NOT in his office when Jael returned from her visit with Melinda Carson. Rabbit explained that Josh had gone to the infirmary to visit with Lieutenant Andrew Carson again and learned the soldier had slipped out of the infirmary during the night. Shortly before dawn he had collected supplies from the quartermaster and retrieved his horse and ridden west. Josh had decided to pursue.

"Why did he do that?" Jael snapped.

"He seems to suspect that the lieutenant killed Mollie Day, and he is afraid the man is going to escape."

"It doesn't matter. I have a witness who will vouch for Broken Wing."

Rabbit beamed. "You do? Then Broken Wing will be freed?"

"It appears so. At least until you spring your trap."

"It is already sprung. He just doesn't know it yet."

"When did Josh leave?"

"Probably two hours ago."

"And he was headed west?"

"Yes, and the doctor, Captain Olson, was with him."

"Why did Captain Olson go with him?"

"He said he knew where the lieutenant might be going. I guess he also felt responsible since the patient was under his care. Josh said the surgeon insisted on going with him. The Army will not do anything because the lieutenant is not absent without leave . . . at least not yet."

The scenario seemed very strange to Jael. Captain Charles Olson did not strike Jael as the type of man inclined to dirty his hands and work up a sweat chasing a soldier who was not technically violating any Army regulation. She found his level of interest in the incident bothersome.

Jael said, "Rabbit, could you stay with Michael tonight? You may take Rylee's room as usual. I will ask Rosa to leave you both something for supper."

"Yes, I can do that. You are going to follow Josh, aren't you?"

"I will try to. I plan to swing by the reservation and see if my friend, Growling Bear, can go with me. He is the best tracker in the Kwahadi band, and he will be very helpful if there is trouble."

"You expect trouble?"

"Possibly double trouble."

Chapter 24

I T FELT RIGHT to Jael to be riding with Growling Bear at her side again. During her Comanche life, he had accompanied her many times on her missions as interpreter and negotiator for Quanah. An unusually tall and burly man for a Comanche, his appearance fit his name, and, while gentleness was his nature, he was fierce in the protection of his cub, the woman he still called She Who Speaks.

After leaving the office, Jael had quickly changed into her doeskin riding britches, shirt and moccasins and snatched up a bag of biscuits and jerky Rosa had packed for her. She hitched her bow and a quiver of arrows to the saddle, and, with her Winchester in its scabbard and Colt in the saddlebags, had nudged Trouble forward at a gallop toward the reservation.

She had not had to sell Growling Bear on the mission. He was not cut out for reservation life and leaped at the opportunity for an adventure. His two wives had been dispatched to pack some pemmican and breads, and in little more than an hour they were searching for Josh's trail. Growling Bear picked up tracks for two riders mounted on shod horses quickly. One of the riders was military, the warrior said. The other was Josh, whom he had tracked on many occasions before the Kwahadi made their dismal trek to the reservation.

They spoke Comanche as they rode. Growling Bear spoke fragments of both English and Spanish, but they were on a quest, like in the old times, and Jael easily shifted into her tribesman's comfortable tongue.

"This is strange," Growling Bear said, "they seem to know their destination because I find no sign of any third rider they might be following."

"The white medicine man said he thought he knew where the third man might be going."

"Is that not strange, also? If a man is running away, why would he tell another where he was going and then wait there to be found. I do not understand the thinking of these white men."

"That is what concerns me. Josh had not heard about the things I learned before he left. He may be trusting a cunning coyote."

"I think these men ride toward Turkey Foot," Growling Bear said. "It is two sunrises from here, less if the rains do not come and the churning clouds do not strike." He pointed toward the southwestern sky that was blackening and sucking away the billowing clouds in the distance in a way that sometimes portended a tornado. Her first thought was of Michael, but she reassured herself he could be in no better hands than Rabbit's. She would know where to find cover if a tornado descended in their direction.

"How much time do we have to find cover?" she asked, knowing that time measured in hours was difficult for Comanche to grasp and that there was no word in the language for the concept.

Growling Bear grimaced and appeared to be considering the question. He looked up and studied the black mass that seemed to be gaining speed as it moved in their direction. He pointed toward a bluff that erupted like a giant molar from the desolate prairie. "From here to there," he said, "if we ride as fast as the wind."

No more words were needed. Instantly, they kneed their mounts in a race for the butte. Jael's gelding pulled out in the lead. She guessed the animal was not only faster than Growling Bear's horse but had the advantage of carrying a hundred pounds less weight. But they pushed the horses to their limits as the darkness consumed the sky, broken only by the roaring thunderbolts of lightning that flashed through the blackness. Just before they reached the shelter of the butte, she saw spinning, twin twisters, perhaps a half-mile distant, kicking the earth and then rising briefly before striking again.

They took cover on the northeast side of the claylike stony butte that stood some thirty feet high and nearly fifty feet wide on their side. Growling Bear located a concave depression at the base that had been carved out by time and elements to form a shelter that would not quite qualify as a cave. They staked their mounts as close to the wall as possible and then hunkered down to wait.

The rain struck first, pouring from the sky in torrents before the winds started whipping around the corners of the formation and clumps of wet clay began sliding down the slope. Jael could barely hear Growling Bear when he yelled for her to grab her horse's reins and hold tight. Darkness swallowed the prairie, although it was the middle of the afternoon, and moments of stillness and silence settled in, seducing her to believe the storm was ending. Then a ferocious roar echoed across the plains, and the winds, even more violent now, erupted and hammered at their shelter. She watched with awe and disbelief as stones and trees flew past as if suddenly endowed with wings. She feared that the butte would begin to crumble and cave in and bury them there.

Just as quickly as the barrage of wind had appeared, it followed the gyrating tornado funnels eastward, leaving behind a steady drought-quenching rain.

"These were not so big," Growling Bear said.

"Big enough," Jael replied. She had seen tornados wreaking havoc on the Texas plains during her years with the Comanche, but she had never been in the monsters' direct path before. "Is it safe for us to ride on?"

"I know a place near a stream and trees that we can reach before the sun sleeps."

"We had just as well ride in the rain as stand still and be drenched. Wet is wet."

They mounted their horses, and Jael fell in behind her Comanche guide as they headed in the direction of the place Growling Bear called Turkey Foot.

Chapter 25

JOSH FIGURED IF he peered into a mirror he would see a fool. After two nights on the trail, they were no more than a mile distant from the landmark canyon known as Turkey Foot. The Llano Estacado, or Great Plains, was broken up in many places by isolated canyons and rock formations that appeared to spontaneously carve out a slice of the earth's surface or thrust above it without warning. He had camped at Turkey Foot a few years earlier on a trip to Fort Sill from the firm's home office in Santa Fe. It had been a pleasant stop. Shade and windbreak from the cottonwoods and oak. Fresh water. Lush grazing for the horses.

In some respects, the place might have been a miniature Palo Duro Canyon, which commenced its journey a few hundred miles southwest. Turkey Foot was a canyon dotted with springs that oozed and dripped water from the canyon walls. It was cleaved by a stream fed by the springs that ran the canyon's two-mile length before branching off into three directions. From the canyon's rim, the stream's split, with a bit of imagination, appeared like a giant turkey's track—hence the canyon's name.

After two nights on the trail, uneasiness with his traveling companion, Captain Charles Olson, had shifted to extreme wariness. The captain's insistence on accompanying him had never made much sense. He was clearly a prima donna accustomed to the finer things of life, mostly provided by his wealthy wife, who had remained back east during the Sill tour of duty. The man had whined like a toddler when the thunderstorm struck night before last, and Josh had converted the canvas tarp that wrapped his bedroll into a serviceable rain shelter to share with his unappreciative companion. Olson had brought no food supplies with him and only a single canteen, forcing Josh to share his own meager rations.

What troubled Josh most was the certainty the surgeon expressed about the whereabouts of their quarry. Why would Lieutenant Andrew Carson seemingly make an escape from Fort Sill but tell someone where to find him? Josh found it difficult to interpret Carson's action as anything but an admission of guilt in the murder of Mollie Day. But Captain Olson fit into this somewhere. The man did not strike him as a good Samaritan, and his interest in Mollie Day's death had earlier seemed no more than professional.

When they reached the mouth of the canyon, it was late morning. Josh said, "There is a lot of canyon here. Plenty of places to hide. You seem to know this guy's itinerary. Where do we find him?"

"We just follow the stream. He'll find us."

"That's what I'm afraid of. We make damn good targets for somebody hidden away in the rocks along the walls."

"He won't shoot me. He thinks I've hidden away something he wants, and he can't locate it if I'm dead."

"That's not much comfort to me. I figured the two of you had an arrangement of some kind."

"I am the lieutenant's reluctant partner, temporarily."

Just before they reached a grove of towering cottonwoods, two rifle shots cracked, and dust kicked up in front of the two riders. Josh yanked his Winchester from its scabbard and dropped from his mount and dived behind one of the trees. His riderless horse galloped upstream. Olson reined in his mount.

"Idiot," the surgeon yelled. "Now the law wrangler's on the loose."

"Did you bring my money?"

The voice came from scrub bushes along the base of the canyon wall, Josh guessed no more than fifty yards away. He was not an accomplished marksman, certainly not one of Jael's prowess, but it would be easy enough for him to take down Olson, who was an easy target. But he did not know how these two fit together yet or the degree of guilt of either.

"Rivers," Olson said, as he slowly dismounted, "come on out here where he can see you. The three of us need to have a chat. We just need to reach an understanding. Negotiate. That's what lawyers do, isn't it?"

"I'll come out if he tosses out his rifle and walks down here with his hands above his head."

"You hear that, Carson. Throw out your rifle and get your butt over here. We'll talk about this."

"I asked you if you brought my money. Five thousand dollars gold double eagles. That's what we agreed on. And I'm not about to throw out my gun."

"I brought the money, but I hid it up the trail. You don't think I would be fool enough to ride in here and let you shoot me and take off with the money? I want to be sure we've got an understanding and that I don't get a bullet in my back."

Josh had not seen the surgeon hide anything and suspected there was no money, but what was this all about? He quickly found out.

"You murdered Mollie, Captain. I saw you leave her quarters. And I saw her body after you left. Then the Indian came along and set up your plan, and, just in case that didn't work out, you had me and Melinda for back-up."

"I didn't kill her. The peyote did. I didn't know what I was doing."

"I just want my money. My military career is done however this turns out. You pay me, and I'm on my way to a new life someplace. I'll just disappear in California. Then there's no witness to tie you to it."

"What about your wife?"

"Hang it on her if they don't kill the Indian for it. I don't care. I'm not chancing her butcher knife again."

Stalemate. Carson hidden in the brush. Olson hunkered behind his horse. Josh behind the trees with a clear shot at Olson's back.

Suddenly, the sound of hooves pounded on the trail they had followed into the canyon. Olson turned toward the noise, and, at that instant Carson emerged from the brush with his rifle aimed at Olson. Josh raised his own Winchester to fire a shot at the lieutenant, but before he could squeeze the trigger, another weapon fired twice, and Carson's knees buckled, and he pitched forward, dropping his rifle as he crumpled on the rocky ground.

Josh turned his eyes toward Olson, who, oblivious now to the rider on the trail, had spun around to identify the source of the gunfire. The diversion cost him because the giant on horseback charged in and with a powerful swing of his stone-headed war club drove the weapon into the side of Olson's head and knocked him senseless.

Growling Bear raised a hand to Josh in greeting as he reined in his mount. A few minutes later, Josh saw his wife kneeling by Carson, who, by the way he was writhing and moaning, was not going to die immediately. What in the hell was she doing here, anyway?

He checked Olson's prone form. The rise and fall of his chest was the sole sign of life in his body. The bone on the right side of his head had caved to Growling Bear's blow, leaving a scarlet, pulpy pit in his skull. Josh wondered if a man ever woke up from something like that. Growling Bear stood back some distance, watching on with expressionless eyes, his face stoic. He turned away and trotted toward Jael when she called to him in Comanche.

Josh pulled the small hunting knife from the sheath on his belt and began slicing strips of cloth from Olson's shirttail. He moistened one with water from the surgeon's canteen and began wiping blood from the flesh about the wound. He was surprised there was not more blood but had no idea whether that might be good or bad in terms of prognosis. He folded a piece of cloth into a compress to place over the wound and then secured it with a strip tied about the skull.

Chapter 26

THEY SAT IN the shade of the cottonwood trees to ponder unraveling the tangled web in which they found themselves. Jael and Growling Bear shared their ample rations with Josh, who obviously had not had much to eat for a day or two. Captain Charles Olson was stretched on a saddle blanket, still unconscious. Lieutenant Carson lay nearby, his head propped up on a bedroll. He would survive if his two thigh wounds did not putrefy, Jael thought. She had shot to disable, not to kill. He was a potential witness, and she hoped he would fill in the gaps in the scenario she had reconstructed. He seemed clear-headed and not in unbearable agony now that she had patched and bound the gunshot wounds. She had not attempted to remove the slugs and would leave that for the surgeons at Sill. It would be a painful journey for the lieutenant.

Growling Bear got up and went into the trees in search of trees or limbs suitable for constructing the two travois they would need for transporting the wounded soldiers. Josh had been strangely silent since her arrival. She recognized the signs. He was miffed at her about something. Best to pluck the thorn than let it fester. "What's stuck in your craw, Joshua?"

He finished off a biscuit and took a swig of water from his canteen before he replied. "I don't know why in hell you took it on yourself to saddle up and take off after me. I'm a grown man in case you hadn't noticed."

"Oh, I've noticed, I promise that. But a bit of the pouty boy comes out from time to time."

"Pouty? What do you mean?"

"You know what I mean. You're sore because I came after you. You see it as an insult to your manhood somehow." She found herself growing more impatient as she spoke. "Well, ordinarily I wouldn't have interfered, but I obtained information you didn't have and realized you were riding after the lieutenant with a killer at your back. You might have ended up dead if we hadn't showed up. And contrary as you can be sometimes, a big part of me would have died with you. I'm not sorry we came, so get over it, Joshua."

Josh grabbed an overhanging cottonwood branch and pulled himself up. He stepped toward her and reached out his hand. She took it, and he pulled her to her feet, and put his arms around her. "You are incredibly beautiful when you're angry. It makes it worth a bit of a whipping."

She lifted her chin, and his lips found hers, and she melted. "Thank you," he said. "For tracking us. For everything."

"In case you haven't noticed, I'm dying over here." It was Lieutenant Andrew Carson's raspy voice.

Jael turned her head and looked at the pale, weak soldier, who lay about five paces away. "Shut up." She placed her hand behind Josh's head and drew his face to hers for another lingering kiss before she stepped away to tend to the patient.

She then knelt beside Carson and checked his improvised dressings. The pant leg had been cut off, and she could see the bleeding from his outer thigh wounds had been staunched to a trickle. His shirt was blood-soaked, however. Evidently, the earlier knife wound had been aggravated by the rough ride to Turkey Foot or his tumble after Jael took him down. She took his shirt off, salvaged what she could and wrapped knotted pieces of the cloth around his chest.

While Jael tended to the wounded lieutenant, Josh asked, "What about Broken Wing's attempted suicide at the guard house? Who smuggled in the rope. Was it you, Carson?"

Jael answered, "It had to be Captain Olson. He visited the guardhouse on the pretense of checking on Broken Wing's condition. I'm certain he had the rope stuffed in his medical bag. He also gave the young man something to help him sleep. It's a fair guess that it was peyote. I suspect he planted a few suggestions in his patient's mind before he departed."

"But Olson could not have been certain Broken Wing would respond the way he planned."

"No, of course not, but he had nothing to lose, and he did consider himself an expert on the substance."

When she finished the patch job, Jael said, "Now we are going to have a serious talk."

"I don't know what you mean," Carson replied.

Josh remained standing and leaned back against a tree trunk.

"I mean you are going to answer some questions," Jael continued. "And if you give the wrong answers, you are a good candidate for a firing squad. We have a witness who will testify Broken Wing did not kill Mollie Day."

"My wife?"

"Yes. She suspects you."

"Me. Why me?"

"Because you were engaged in, shall we say, 'intimate transactions' with her sister, and you were jealous of her other clients and outraged when you learned of her relationship with Broken Wing."

"That's not true. I don't know anything about a relationship with the Indian. And I sure wasn't jealous. I was claiming a percent of her revenues to keep quiet. I even arranged some business."

"Was Captain Olson a part of the business you arranged?"

Carson hesitated. "Yes. And he was the one who became jealous and possessive. He wanted her exclusively. He received a generous allowance from his wife who lived back east, and most of it went to Mollie."

"Less your cut."

"If you say so."

"So why did Captain Olson kill Mollie?"

"I didn't say that."

"It's down to you and the Captain."

"Okay. He did it. Mollie turned him down the previous night. Said she was going out of business. He didn't take it well. He was interested in the Peyote Religion and maintained a supply of the buttons . . . for medicinal purposes, he said. He chewed peyote the night of the killing, he told me, and was told by the spirit Mollie had to be sacrificed. He went to her quarters and raped her. Then he cut her throat."

"What about the other wounds?"

"A second thought. He was concerned that the knife wound was too precise . . . looked too premeditated. He did the other mutilation to make it look more like an act of anger or rage."

"And his action was not?"

"Not in his twisted mind. He saw it as a matter of obedience to a higher force."

"How do you know all of this if you were not a co-conspirator?"

"I guessed that he was the killer. He came to me several times that day to intercede with Mollie. He was very agitated. I just wanted her to leave the post quietly. I was afraid my wife already knew . . . or would soon. My military career was at risk if this turned to scandal. After Mollie's death, I thought it was all over, but Broken Wing conveniently showed up."

"And you were willing to let him die."

"He was just an Indian."

"I see." But she did not. "But then you saw that the investigation was not ended."

"Yes. You and your husband were asking too many questions, and I realized my involvement in so many ways was turning me into an alternate suspect. No matter what happened, my career looked like it was in the latrine. I went to Olson and told him I knew he did it, although I wasn't certain. I said if he would give me five thousand dollars, I would leave the post and disappear. That's when he said he was sorry and went into the gibberish about some outside force making him do it. He promised to pay me, but said he needed time. A few days later, I ended up in the hospital, and I was afraid he would kill me there, especially when I learned he was giving me that peyote crap."

"Is that why you decided to escape?"

"Partly. But Olson came to me before that and put forth the idea. He said I should meet him at Turkey Foot, and he would give me the money. I'm sure he didn't bring it. He would have needed more time to come up with it. But I grabbed for the bait because I didn't want to stay in the infirmary under his supervision. And I did not want to go to sleep in my quarters with my wife there. I ran and decided to take my chances with the money. I knew he would possibly be coming out here to kill me, but I still had hope of seeing the money. I didn't expect him to bring company."

"You will be required to testify about this."

"It's the truth. I'll get drummed out of the Army. Maybe some guardhouse time. They won't shoot me for it."

Jael looked over at Olson, who remained in deep slumber. "I don't know if anybody will get shot for it."

Chapter 27

TWO DAYS AFTER their return to Fort Sill, Josh and Jael sat in General Mackenzie's office. The general pulled thoughtfully at his moustache. "Both of you are here. I doubt it's a social call. But your client, Broken Wing, has been released from the guardhouse. I saw him yesterday leading a string of horses and heading in the direction of your place. In fact, he was accompanied by the little lady who works in your office . . . Bunny, is it?"

"Rabbit," Jael corrected.

"And I've bought your theory about the multiple wives for now. It should hold until I vacate this godforsaken place. But you know this isn't the end of that story."

"We do." Josh said, "And we'd like to assure Quanah that the Army's not going to crack down on the Peyote Religion anytime soon."

"So, you're tying up some loose ends for your important client. That's what this is about?" Mackenzie was frugal with his smiles, but he surrendered a small closed-lipped one. "I suppose you can't submit a bill until you've given him a positive report."

Mackenzie was closer to the truth than he realized, Josh thought. "The Army's got an interest in this," Josh pointed out. "The senior surgeon using peyote in treatments and then allegedly killing someone while under its influence."

"This borders on extortion," Mackenzie said.

"Captain Olson's regained consciousness now," Josh said, "but your doctors say he doesn't know who he is or where he's at. Just babbles. They don't think he'll ever do much more than that."

"Can't do a court martial in that condition. It would have been cheaper if that horse kick would have killed him . . . by the way, one of the surgeons doesn't believe that injury was caused by a horse kick."

Jael and Josh gave simultaneous shrugs. They had agreed it would be best to limit Growling Bear's role in their narrative, and Lieutenant Carson had not witnessed the striking of the war club.

"About the peyote . . . " Josh said.

"To hell with it. The Army's got no orders to deal with it. Let the preachers fret about it. Hands off from the Army's standpoint . . . for now. Just like the wives. Now get out of here and write up your bill for Quanah, if you don't have anything better to do."

They got up and strolled out of the office. Outside, Jael said. "I was just thinking."

"What?"

"Michael's staying out at the reservation tonight, and Rabbit's probably already locked up the office. So I can think of something better to do than billing."

Josh looked at her. She smiled impishly. They raced for the carriage.